D0058368

Hodges, Hollis
Don't tell me your name.

DATE DUE

Ja 20 '79	Ap 13 '79	Nov 24 '79	Apr 6 '81
Ja 23 '79	AP 24 '79	Nov 24 '79	Jul 6 '81
Ja 31 '79			Jul 29 '81
	May 19 '79	De 29 '79	May 1 '82
	May 31 '79	Ja 16 '80	Jul 1 '82
Fe 8 '79	Je 18 '79	Mar 8 '80	Jul 14 '82
Fe 14 '79	Jul 9 '79	Mar 18 '80	Dec 10 '83
Mr 19 '79	Dec 25 '79	Mar 27 '80	Aug 22 '84
Mar 26 '79	Nov 7 '79	Dec 3 '80	Mar 18 '85
	No 12 '79	Feb 19 '81	

Don't Tell Me Your Name

Don't Tell Me Your Name

A NOVEL BY

Hollis Hodges

CROWN PUBLISHERS, INC., NEW YORK

*Any resemblance of characters in this novel to persons
living or dead is purely coincidental.*

Inquiries should be addressed to Crown Publishers, Inc.,
One Park Avenue, New York, N.Y. 10016

Printed in the United States of America
Published simultaneously in Canada by
General Publishing Company Limited

Book Design: Huguette Franco

Library of Congress Cataloging in Publication Data

Hodges, Hollis.
Don't tell me your name.
I. Title.
PZ4.H688Do   1978   [PS3558.03434]   813'.5'4   78-17235
ISBN 0-517-53472-X

TO JEFF AND FRAN

"Life isn't all winning," he said. "One of the things you got to learn is to be able to lose."

He said, "Like sometimes you get a pencil sharpened to just the right point and you set it on the table and it falls off and rolls behind the radiator."

1

Although they probably wouldn't admit it, most of the adult males in the town of Munsen, Massachusetts, envied Toomey Bougereau. And they didn't envy him because of his youth, wealth, family background, good looks, talent, or social position.

He ranked low to medium in all those categories.

The adult males of Munsen envied Toomey Bougereau because he owned a small basket-weaving business called Baskets and Baskets and appeared to have his own little harem of four or five, usually five, good-looking women working for him. Young liberated women, mostly. Blue jeans and long hair. Always, people pointed out, so attractive and well built that you had to assume that those characteristics most surely had been taken into account as part of the hiring process.

On days when the weather was warm enough, you could see his young women playing Frisbee on the grass in front of the building. Barefoot, bare legs, bare midriffs. Bending over, leaping high, loping gracefully across the lawn. Stretching, bending, laughing, and shouting. Enjoying. Almost enough to make a man on his way to or from lunch go a block or more out of his way just to happen to be passing by.

There were, however, among those who did not envy Mr. Bougereau, some who were actually hostile toward him. A number of people, mostly wives and the elderly unmarried, felt that the town would be better off without Bougereau and his loose young women. With the exception of Mrs. Murphey, a local woman who was well known and highly respected, the employees of Baskets and Baskets were thought of as hippie types from the eastern part of the state or New York City.

Mrs. Walter Carew was one such person. She would like to have seen Bougereau's place closed down. She told everyone how she had gone there once to apply for a job and had been turned down because Mr. Bougereau had thought she wasn't young and sexy enough.

She also reported that he had been drinking.

Mr. Collins, the mailman, who has been delivering mail along Main Street for nearly twenty-five years, said that he was almost afraid to go near the place. He said that the young women always came running up to see if there was any mail for them and they were usually only half dressed. And a mailman has enough hardships and obstacles to face as he makes his appointed rounds without having three or four young women without much of anything on come crowding around the moment he walks in the door.

It was Mr. Collins who reported that Toomey had a couch in his office.

Not a couch, really. More like a bed. And Toomey didn't look like the kind of man who took a nap in the afternoon.

A nip, maybe. But not a nap.

Toomey Bougereau was a thirty-eight-year-old man who had come from somewhere out of state. From somewhere in Connecticut, people said. He had shown up here in December, for some reason having decided that this was where he was going to settle for a while. The fact that he wanted to settle down here was not in itself especially unusual, inasmuch as quite often people from out of town come to Munsen and fall in love with the place, its beauty and tranquility, and decide to stay. People know that everyone who comes up here from New York City for the summer finds it very difficult to return to the city in the fall. But John Harvey, who talked with Toomey when he first came to town, reported that it was his feeling that Toomey had come to Munsen to stay, even before he'd seen what the place looked like.

That was strange.

Someone said they'd learned that he'd been twice married and twice divorced. Which in itself was enough to cause the people of Munsen to question his morality and respectability.

Bougereau stayed in town a little less than a year. And during that period a number of people made life difficult for him. A judge in Boston, father of one of the young women who worked at Baskets and Baskets, for one. A young social worker from Farmington, for another. Plus the members of a motorcycle gang called The Hornets, a worker for the Munsen Highway Department, several members of the local post of the Veterans of Foreign Wars, and a religious organization called Christian Bounty.

Some of these even felt that they helped speed his departure from the town.

Toomey would have laughed at the idea that any of those people or organizations, or even all of them combined, could have driven him out of town if he hadn't been ready to go. He would happily have taken them on one at a time or all of them together.

It turned out that the person who drove Toomey Bougereau out of town was a woman.

He thought she was beautiful. And he loved her very much.

Toomey Bougereau loved that woman as much as any man anywhere has ever loved a woman.

That's the way it is, sometimes.

Toomey was a big man, six feet four, overweight by about twenty pounds, probably, with brown eyes and facial features arranged in a standard sort of way. He had a goodly amount of dark hair that looked as if it pretty much took care of itself. Ordinarily his expression ranged from relatively undisturbed to downright placid. Good teeth and eyesight, far as that goes. Big feet, as people often noticed and joked about. He was in good health, and moved a little faster than you would expect of a man his size.

Prominent among his better memories were three years as left tackle for the Wildcats of Angora High School in Angora, Indiana. All-Valley in his junior year. And captain of the team his senior year, the year the Wildcats won the state championship.

Because Toomey was a fisherman, a few of the older sportsmen in town defended him against his critics. He must have some good qualities, they said. Any man who goes out in the early evening in an old rowboat with a dog on the back seat of the boat and sometimes uses minnows and worms and a big red bobber can't be all bad. And if you happen to be casting lures from the shore and get a line snagged on a branch or log he'll row over to where your lure is snagged and get the line loose for you. Which is a nice thing to do and the sign of a good sportsman and good neighbor.

The town, some people said, could use a few more people like him. Especially if you used lures and fished from the shore.

One of his mother's best friends back in Angora had been a woman named Madeline Toomey, a seamstress and part-time fortune teller who died two days before Toomey was born. Which explains how he got his rather unusual first name. In memoriam.

Whether he had also inherited that good woman's psychic gifts was a matter of conjecture. Toomey, himself, was never really certain one way or the other. It did so happen, however, that as the years went by Toomey got pretty good at sewing on buttons and mending his own clothes. And there was a noticeable tendency on his part to analyze people, figure out what they'd been like in earlier years, and predict their future.

Only last year, at a time when it seemed that everything in his life had gone wrong, he had sewn up a rip in his coat and gone to the racetrack and after gazing into an upside-down shot glass had picked four winners out of seven.

Which isn't bad.

His mother had once told Toomey that while she was pregnant with him, Madeline had predicted that the unborn child would be a healthy and handsome boy who would grow up to be wealthy, famous, and happy. And that he would care and provide for her in her old age.

All of which was very nice, except that her predictions turned out to be less than 100 percent accurate.

His mother hadn't even reached old age.

And as for Toomey's becoming wealthy and famous, he had so far not achieved either and did not consider it likely that he would achieve either in the near or distant future.

(Years ago he had seen the possibility—probability, even—of becoming wealthy. But that had been years ago.)

Had he found happiness?

Real happiness?

Well, once. For a brief time. A day. And one day of happiness in the life of a thirty-eight-year-old man isn't enough to justify saying that even that small part of Madeline's prediction had come true.

What Madeline had predicted for his older sister and two brothers, he didn't know. But he doubted that she had predicted for the boys that the oldest would be killed in an automobile accident while still in high school and that the other would die fighting in the Korean War. Or that his sister would have three sets of twin girls in a row and get her picture in the Indianapolis *Sunday Star*.

His sister's name was Ethel. She was older than Toomey by eight years. She was happily married to a man who owned a TV sales and repair shop and had three hunting dogs and four guns and six daughters.

Toomey hadn't seen much of his sister in recent years, but lately he had got into the habit of calling her on the phone every couple of weeks. He'd ask her what was happening in Angora these days, and she'd ask when was he going to quit that basket-weaving foolishness and go back to work.

He'd ask how was the fishing, and she'd say that she also thought he ought to cut back on his drinking.

As far as he knew, she was the only relative he had.

The year-round population of Munsen, according to the federal census, is only fifteen hundred and twenty-eight. Which is only one hundred and two more than it was ten years ago.

The town is noted for nothing. Except, possibly, the fact that there are two nearly identical lakes here, one on each side of the highway, which, legend has it, were man-made by a famous Indian chief many years ago as identical wedding gifts for his two beautiful twin daughters. But only if you are from out of town or real drunk could you ever believe a story like that.

George Munsen, after whom the town was named, was an early settler who once owned all the land hereabouts and who figures prominently in the history of the region. He had numerous offspring, all of whom have become successful and all of whom have left the area. And although the Munsen name is well known in western Massachusetts, with one representative in the state legislature, one judge, and several who are prominent lawyers or doctors, no one with the last name of Munsen today lives in the town of that name.

Every once in a while someone says that they think the town should be re-named Twin Lakes. But people point out that George Munsen is a famous historical figure and that no one even knows the name of the famous Indian chief who supposedly built the lakes. And besides, most of the lake property now is owned by people from Boston or New York who come here only during the summer months with their noisy power-boats and their spoiled kids.

The hills surrounding Munsen are beautiful. Gently rolling, heavily wooded. Green or brown or bright red and yellow, depending upon the time of year. Some of that wide expanse of forest appears at a distance to be so unscarred and unblemished that you could easily believe that there are parts of it where no human being has ever intruded.

Nick Nicocci, the Munsen chief of police, pointed out that fact to Toomey one afternoon in early August. He was in uniform, was on official duty, and was even wearing his gun and holster.

Nicocci was a member of one of the town's best-known families. One brother had the town's only barber shop and another the town's only liquor store. Nick occasionally helped out at both places. He was short, thin, had sharp features, and looked hard. Which he wasn't. He was a good father and husband, had a large family, liked to hunt and fish. Hated arresting anyone.

They were standing in the parking lot of Baskets and Baskets, looking toward the lake and beyond. Nick made a large sweeping gesture that took in the wide range of hills that filled the background.

He said, "You see all those woods? Those thick woods where no one ever goes? Where maybe no one has ever been?"

Toomey nodded. He saw them. Hundreds and hundreds of acres of solid forest, probably.

Nick said, "You realize that that young woman's body could be up there somewhere and maybe not be discovered for years and years?"

They both thought about that in silence for a moment.

"Maybe never?"

Toomey filled his pipe, spilling a little tobacco as he did so.

Nick said, "That's why I'm not asking for a thousand volunteers to start searching the woods."

Toomey was glad to hear that. He nodded his approval.

"You're right, Nick. I think that's a wise decision."

Without taking his eyes from the range of thick green hills, looking grim and unsmiling, Nick shook loose a cigarette from the pack and lit it.

"It would be like looking for a needle in a haystack."

"That's true," Toomey said. "Very true."

"It would be a waste of time."

2

Except for the twin lakes, Munsen, Massachusetts, is much like every other town in the United States.

Water runs downhill. Taxes go up. People are born, live, and die. In the spring, seedlings from the damp earth reach out toward the warm sun. And in the autumn, leaves fall and people gather the harvest in and put up storm windows and check the wood supply. Birds fly above the ground and moles and earthworms burrow beneath it. The six o'clock news starts promptly at six o'clock on all three major TV networks. And Saturday at twelve sharp the fire department tests its siren and scares hell out of the tourists eating lunch across the street at Harvey's.

People laugh and people cry. Stars come out at night, the moon changes shape, seasons move along in their orderly fashion. Kids get on and off the school bus. People go to work and in most cases return. Lovers quarrel and make up. Or don't. A woman in one part of town comes home from the hospital to find the house so crowded with proud grandparents that you can hardly find room to change the baby's diapers. And in another place a woman comes back alone to an empty house and cries bitterly and questions how God could be so cruel as to let a baby die before it had even drawn a first breath.

Some win, some lose. The bus pulls away from in front of Harvey's Variety Store and there's almost always someone who got there too late. Which is too bad for them, because there are only two buses a day. But sometimes that gives Charlie's Taxi Service a chance to make a couple bucks. So that's good for him.

A man in town sells his old car because he needs money to pay his daughter's hospital bill and doesn't tell the boy who bought it that the clutch is shot. And kids find dimes on the sidewalk sometimes, and once in a long while a wallet. With money in it.

People grow old alone, sometimes. Perhaps by only minutes having missed meeting that person with whom they could have lived happily all their lives. Maybe. And golden wedding anniversaries take place here in about the same proportion per capita as in the rest of the United States. People go off to war and do or don't return in about the same proportion as everywhere else. And the amount of money won at the Saturday night poker game at the VFW is exactly the same as the amount of money lost.

Mrs. Estey, the rather plain middle-aged woman behind the counter at the luncheonette, stuffs in her pocket the phone number the truck driver left next to his plate, and tells herself that the next time Ed calls and says that he has to work late again she'll do something other than just cry. And Johnny Malloy, who manages the Florsheim shoe store in Farmington, brings flowers and candy home to the woman he's loved and been married to for ten years and she tells him and the children that it's such a happy birthday that she could almost cry.

And does, a little.

People are carrying on in other parts of the country, too.

In Boston, a respected and influential elderly statesman gets back to the office, grins, winks, and locks the door so that he and his attractive young secretary won't be interrupted for a while. And even farther away, in Washington, D.C., a young aide to the President is planning to lay a certain young member of the household staff quickly across a certain bed in the White House the next time the First Family leaves on vacation or on official business. Which may come as early as this next weekend. And then they'll both have a story that they can use as a conversation stopper at any cocktail party or bar anywhere in the country.

And at one bar in the country, the Edgewood Lounge in Rye, New York, a tired businessman slides onto a stool and shakes his head and asks for a double Manhattan on the rocks. When the man next to him asks why the pained look, he explains that his wife, backing the car in her usual careless fashion out of the parking lot at Lord & Taylor's, backed right over a kid's bike.

The man says that he doesn't think that was so bad. "Unless the kid was still on it."

"He wasn't." And he takes a long sip of his drink.

"Then cheer up. Kids' bikes aren't that expensive."

He says, "You think not? A Honda Automatic?"

In Baldwinsville, Connecticut, a Dr. Creighton is hosting an afternoon cocktail party for the professional staff and selected guests from the town and university. The party is being held on the terrace. The sun is shining, there is a gentle breeze, and everyone agrees that it is an ideal day for an outdoor gathering. The guests are enjoying themselves, the food is excellent, the drinks good, and the conversation sparkling. Dr. Creighton and his daughter, Gertrude, are delighted at how well everything is going.

The occasion is the twenty-eighth anniversary of the Creighton Medical Center, a small institution serving the emotionally ill, primarily through the use of psychoanalysis, group therapy, occupational therapy, and what Dr. Creighton refers to as a health and growth milieu. Its patients are mostly attractive and intelligent young members of wealthy families. They were selected from a long waiting list. Seldom is one selected who is potentially violent or whose emotional problems are of a gross or distasteful nature. And none of them, of course, would be at this particular party anyway.

The reputation of the center is now firmly established in medical and psychoanalytic circles, and the credit for this is given to that person to whom it undeniably belongs, the host of this party, Dr. Elton Creighton.

A little later on, his daughter, Gertrude, will say something in that regard when she presents a long toast in tribute to her father, who caused all this to come to be.

Gertrude, it might be noted, is herself an analyst.

Off to one side, a Dr. Larmouth, talking to a colleague who had only recently joined the staff, was reminiscing about a member of the staff who had worked here some years ago and whom he remembered with respect and affection.

"I recall a few years back, at a party something like this, that Gertrude was raving about how wonderful Bettelheim's new book was. The one about the meaning and importance of fairy tales. You familiar with the book?"

His colleague nodded. "I read it."

"He disagreed, of course. As you would expect. At that stage of their marriage, he and Gertrude were disagreeing on about everything."

He continued. "Anyway, he said that maybe fairy tales had given Bettelheim moral and emotional sustenance, but that they hadn't had that effect on him. He said that, far as he knew, the only thing he'd got out of fairy tales was that one should know better than to kiss a frog because it might turn into a handsome prince."

They laughed for a moment.

"What did Gertrude say to that?"

"At first," Larmouth said, "she just looked at him in that cold, critical way she has. Then she told him flatly that his remark only revealed his subconscious fear of latent homosexuality."

Later, Dr. Larmouth's friend asked him what had ever happened to Bougereau, anyway.

"After he and Gertrude split up," Larmouth said, "Toomey

went someplace in Connecticut, I understand, and worked at some boys' reform school. Still having a private practice on the side. Then he got married again, and that didn't last."

He said, "I heard not long ago that someone said he'd ended up in a small town in Massachusetts somewhere and wasn't practicing anymore."

That was hard to believe. That he would no longer be practicing the profession he had been trained for.

"Why would a man do that?"

Larmouth, of course, didn't know. But he made a guess.

"A woman, I suppose."

A little later Larmouth said, "He should have stayed here. He could have been running the place in a few years."

He added, "I wish he were here now. We could use someone here with a sense of humor."

His colleague agreed with that.

In Coultraine, Massachusetts, a middle-aged salesman for Armand's Paper Products waited at Mike's Garage for his car to be repaired. He had brought the car in because the windshield wipers weren't working and it had started to rain. He sat in the waiting room reading magazines and trying to think up some interesting or funny stories to tell his customers that afternoon. On a rainy day like this you can always use an amusing anecdote to help break the ice. Something funny that had happened to you along the way.

He looked up and saw that apparently the car was going to be ready sooner than he had expected. A mechanic had come from the service area into the room and was saying something to the man he had assumed was Mike, the owner. Something about windshield wiper parts and a half hour of labor. He couldn't hear much of it. But he saw Mike writing down some figures on the sheet.

The salesman stood up. Then he took a second look. And he knew immediately that he had a story that would get him through this day, at least.

The mechanic, standing there in that dirty pair of overalls, wiping those hands on a greasy towel, was a woman.

She was a tall woman, slender, long hair pulled together and tied at the back. A thin, very interesting face. All in all, not bad looking.

And this was the punch line. That woman was as pregnant as any woman he'd seen for a long time. He'd be willing to bet that she was six or seven months along.

He almost couldn't believe his eyes. He watched as she turned and left the office.

Mike, a thin, balding man with an unlit cigar in one corner of his mouth, finished his figuring and waved the papers in the air.

"Your car's ready."

The salesman pulled out his billfold and walked up to the desk.

He said, "Say, wasn't that mechanic a woman?"

Mike said, "Far as I know." And pushed the piece of paper across the counter.

"Nineteen dollars and twenty-one cents."

The man with the cigar was Mike Murphey. He had owned and operated the garage for the last eight years. He was fifty-six years old, a registered Democrat, and once had had his jaw broken by a police officer during an antiwar demonstration in Boston in 1966. He was married, lived in Coultraine, and had two grown sons, neither of whom he had seen for ten years.

The salesman's name was Harry Benson. He had been born in Springfield, Massachusetts, and now lived in Holyoke. He was married and had a son and daughter, both married. He lived with his wife in the Wedgewood Apartments on Bellevue Boulevard. He had worked for Armand's Paper Products for only six months. Before that he had worked for Western Massachusetts Tobacco Wholesalers.

The mechanic's name was Toni Heller. She had been born and raised in Munsen, but now lived in Coultraine. She wasn't married and had only one child. She lived in a large house on Orchard Street with three other women. They shared expenses, divided up the chores, got along as well as people usually do.

14

Better, perhaps. They had their own rooms and their own interests, and occasionally someone moved out to get married or someone moved in after splitting from a man. Everything considered, not a bad arrangement for a woman trying to raise a child by herself. The kid, in fact, was almost getting spoiled from all the attention she got from the other women in the house.

But Toni thought that that was all right. It was her opinion that kids deserved a lot of attention.

She had worked for her Uncle Mike for three years. Almost three and a half years.

And, as Harry Benson had noticed, she was pregnant, all right.

3

Baskets and Baskets was located in a long one-story building on West Main Street. It was the last building that could be considered part of the main business district. Just beyond the Shell gas station. Faded red shingles and peeling white trim. At the west end of the property was a large parking lot. Toomey's office was at that end of the building. Next to his office was a large storage room with supplies and materials along one wall and rows of neatly stacked attractive baskets along the other. The rest of the building, nearly half of it, was one large room crowded with coils of fiber, rope, scraps of wood, a bench with a saw, and a number of women sitting around a long low table more or less weaving baskets. There was always a general air of confusion and disor-der, from out of which, rather surprisingly, came a steady flow of a limited variety of small finished baskets to add to the number already stacked in the other room.

　　At the far end of the work area was a large red and white

cooler with cans of soft drinks on ice, compliments of the boss. And a sink and bathroom, both of which were in good working condition, neither of which was cleaned on any regular schedule. And in the parking lot was a large, eight-year-old, badly dented, blue Dodge van that Toomey loaded with baskets at least once a week, sometimes twice, for delivery to his wholesaler in Boston.

Behind the building there was a narrow and rather steep path leading down to the lake, some three hundred yards away. At the edge of the lake was an old and unpainted rowboat tied to an old and unpainted dock. The rowboat was in pretty good shape, but the dock could use either some new planks or some nails pounded into the old ones.

Earlier in the summer, anyone passing by in the early evening who happened to go by chance out of his way enough to stroll into the parking lot of Baskets and Baskets and chanced to glance down toward the lake would have seen a number of young females diving from the dock and yelling and splashing about in the water. No longer, however. Toomey would not let them swim there anymore. He had ruled that they either had to wear bathing suits or go somewhere else to swim. He told them that they were attracting too much attention. Townspeople were complaining about there being nudity practically right in the middle of Munsen. And you can't have that kind of thing in a community that depends upon the tourist trade for a large part of its summer income.

So now they went to the old quarry off Boyington Road after work, where they could swim without clothes on.

They always asked Toomey if he'd like to join them, but he never did. Though it sounded like fun. And he'd enjoy it, he said. But a lot of the very young people from the area went there and some of them, he thought, would feel uncomfortable at having someone his age there. And he didn't want to spoil it for them.

Baskets and Baskets had the reputation of being a fun place to work, and there was never any difficulty in finding young women who wanted to work there. But turnover was high. With the exception of Mrs. Murphey, who had been with Toomey from the beginning, the longest anyone had stayed had been two and a half months. One had stayed only a week. During the six months that he had now been in business, he had had thirteen women working for him.

Weaving baskets all day gets tiresome, even though there is good conversation, music on the radio, free soda, and nice people to work with. It is a good job for someone who needs to work for a few weeks in order to get enough cash together for some particular purpose. Like money for hiking equipment, a tent, or used car, or maybe just to help out the boyfriend you're living with who is temporarily out of work. And to have a little money saved before you and he start hitching to San Francisco in the fall.

Toomey finished the basket he was working on, and on the way to his office added it to one of the stacks in the storage room.

In his office he was welcomed by a grown dog and a small child, both sprawled on the bare wooden floor. The dog was a large dog of uncertain ancestry and was named Roman. He thumped his tail on the floor several times but didn't bother to get up.

His color was reddish brown with small streaks of black scattered in no particular pattern. He looked as if he'd just moments ago come out of a muddy pond and hadn't yet shaken himself. His head was large in proportion to the rest of his body and he seemed to tire easily and sleep a lot. But if you spoke to him he thumped his tail to let you know that he wasn't really sleeping, only resting.

The child was a four-year-old dark-haired little human being named Myra. She looked up when she heard the door open, saw who it was, and turned back to her coloring book. She studied the picture carefully, then selected what she thought would be the most suitable color, and made a number of large swirls atop the outline of a boy sitting on the edge of a pond holding out a fishing pole.

She said, "Ice cream."

He said, "Paper napkins."

Toomey walked over to his desk and dropped himself into

the worn and scratched leather swivel chair. Another of his purchases from the Goodwill Store in Farmington.

He slid an ashtray toward him, and pulled a small stack of correspondence a little closer.

The child checked to see if the yellow swirls covered the area to her satisfaction. She studied it carefully for a long moment, decided that it did. So she turned to a new page.

Toomey stretched himself, settled a little more comfortably into the chair, and reluctantly reached out and took the top letter from the pile. It was from someone wanting to sell him something. He decided, even before reading it, that he didn't want to buy what they were selling, and tossed it somewhat toward the wastebasket.

He said, "Shoe laces."

The girl hesitated a few seconds, then said, "Candy bar."

And Toomey said, "Well, that was a little slow. But I'll let it go this time."

After all, she was only four. And this was a tough game.

They had made it up a few days ago while walking back from Harvey's.

The way you played it was that one person would name something that was sold at Harvey's. If it was something that you could eat, the other person had to name something right away that you couldn't eat. Or the other way around. And if he or she took too much time in naming something, they lost a point.

He unwrapped a cigar and looked out the window toward the lake.

It was late afternoon and very warm. Too hot for fishing tonight, probably. Unless it cooled off a lot after sunset.

As usual, the lake was filled with motorboats, and Toomey spent a minute or so watching them make their seemingly interminable trips back and forth from one end of the lake to the other. Like wild creatures restlessly pacing the length of their cage. Or rubber balls bouncing themselves against opposite walls. Or something.

He took a quick look at the rest of the mail, decided that none of it looked important enough to bother with on a hot day like this, and pushed the pile of papers off to one side.

He leaned back in the chair again, lit the cigar, and turned on the radio. Just in time to learn that he had missed the national news but that he would be given the regional and local news provided he stayed tuned for an important message.

He reported that fact to Roman and Myra. "We're too late for the national news," he said, "but just in time for an important message."

The radio station was WFRM in Farmington. Twelve miles away. Largest town in the area and the county seat.

The news wasn't exciting, but he passed it along anyway.

"Zayre's is having a big sale," he said. "And Christian Bounty is buying the old Stockwell Inn here in Munsen. The one that closed down last January."

Zayre's was a discount department store. Christian Bounty was a religious organization. The former had been around for years, but the latter was new on the scene. Last year Christian Bounty had bought the old Hulman Academy, a private prep school that had gone bankrupt two years ago. They had converted the old school, with its hundreds of acres and dozen or more buildings, into a religious school and community. And were thriving. Apparently they had almost unlimited financial resources because they were buying up every building in town that was for sale. Mostly for use as dormitory space.

The organization already had over three hundred students, faculty members, or employees who were registered voters. Which caused considerable concern among the citizens of Munsen. The total voter registration in town prior to Christian Bounty's arrival had been only eight hundred and thirty-seven. If the religious group kept growing it would end up not only owning a large part of the town, but would be a decisive factor in all local elections.

"They say that Christian Bounty has not yet decided whether to keep the inn as an investment or to convert it into dormitory space."

He said, "If you believe that, Roman, thump your tail eight times."

Roman opened his eyes part way and thumped his tail three times. And went back to sleep.

The announcer was now going down the list of obituary notices. He concluded with, "And, finally, Mrs. Hartwell, of

Hillsburg, died yesterday at the Springdale Nursing Home."

The announcer provided more details, but Toomey passed along only the basic facts.

"Poor Mrs. Hartwell finally died," he said. "She was eighty-seven and was born in West Plainfield."

Roman thumped his tail twice.

Myra said, "Salt" and Toomey said, "Pepper."

Then he said, "Damn!" And hit his hand on the table. "That's the second time you got me with that."

He took a pencil and made a mark beneath her name on the wall.

"That makes the score sixteen to three, your favor."

Myra was the granddaughter of Mrs. Murphey. She had dark hair, dark eyes, was slender and tall for her age, with a bright and independent look on her face. About once a month she came to visit for a week with her grandmother. Her mother, who lived in Coultraine, dropped her off on Sunday, apparently, and picked her up the following weekend.

Toomey had bought an old couch secondhand from the Goodwill store so Myra would have a place for her afternoon nap. When she wasn't napping or wandering about the shop or helping her grandmother make baskets, she and Toomey would entertain each other. In one corner of the office, in addition to the tall stack of coloring books, there was a box of miscellaneous toys such as building blocks, small cars, and trucks, a couple of Raggedy Ann dolls, and a board with holes in it for pegs of different colors and shapes.

Toomey got out of his chair, went over to where she was working, and got down on his knees to see how she was doing.

He said, "Hey, good! You didn't get too much in between the lines. Only a little bit."

He asked if he could show it to Roman and she said all right. So he held it up so the dog could see it.

"If you think that's pretty good," he said, "thump your tail twice."

Roman thumped his tail four times.

Toomey gave the coloring book back to Myra and patted her

on the head. "Good work." Then he moved back to his desk, opened a drawer, and took out a bottle of bourbon. He poured a little bit into a paper cup, such a small amount that it really didn't count.

He leaned back, took a small sip, and smiled.

Things could be worse.

Myra started a new page, using a different color and temporarily abandoning the swirl technique for the variations on a straight line theme.

Toomey gave a large contented sigh and said to Roman, "The kid's got talent."

Roman thumped his tail again, stretched, then shifted position.

"I remember," Toomey said, "when she couldn't draw anything but a straight line."

The day Myra's grandmother first brought her to the shop, she had come into Toomey's office and stood across the room looking at him with suspicion. Not that she was either frightened or shy, but because he was just too big for her to deal with right away.

She wasn't afraid of Roman, and after a while she sat next to him. And kept an eye on Toomey from that strategic location.

Toomey didn't know whether or not she was too young for crayons, but he went down to Harvey's and bought a dozen coloring books and two boxes of crayons. And showed her how to use them.

He wasn't especially happy about her early work, and told her so.

He said, "You're too conservative."

He said, "You use a crayon like it was the last one you had and it's twelve miles to the nearest store. With snow four feet deep and hostile Indians."

He showed her. "Look. You got to use lots of color. Different colors. And sometimes you break one." And the one he was using happened to break at just that moment.

He tossed the broken crayon in the general direction of the wastebasket.

"That's a dumb color anyway," he said. "I never did like

23

brown." And he took a bright red from the box and gave it to her.

"And when that breaks or you get tired of it, use another color. Use lots of colors."

Another thing he told her. "And just color the pages you want to color. Don't feel you have to color every page just because it's in the book." He gestured toward the stack of coloring books in the corner.

"And there's more where those came from."

Something else she liked to do was sharpen pencils. Sometimes she would occupy herself at that task for twenty minutes. So he had bought a couple dozen of Harvey's less expensive ones.

Anyone with even minimal powers of observation could spot right away that Toomey had no doubt the shortest but sharpest pencils in town.

Maybe in the whole county.

He said, "Newspaper."

After a moment, she said, "Chewing gum."

4

It was true that Toomey Bougereau had been married twice. The first time was while he was still attending Indiana University. To Gertrude Creighton, an attractive, intelligent, scholarly, and hard-working young woman from Baldwinsville, Connecticut. Her father was Dr. Elton Creighton, founder and now director of the Creighton Medical Center, a small private sanitarium for the emotionally ill. He was a widower and she was his only child.

She and Toomey had met in a sophomore psychology class. The professor, a brilliant young Ph.D. from Harvard, had paired the students into teams of two and had assigned each team a project. He had explained to the class that he had done this so that the students could learn to work with others as part of a team. Experimental psychology is largely teamwork, he had said. They should get used to that now.

Nothing could possibly have delighted Toomey more than

to be teamed up with Gertrude. She was exactly the teammate he would have chosen. He had fallen in love with her the first time he'd seen her on that first day of class. He had spent large portions of every classroom period since then wishing that he had the courage to go up to her and say hello. But he was certain that someone like her, beautiful, popular, with poise and style, would not be interested in someone like him.

She was not the most brilliant member of the class. In fact, she had to struggle to keep up with the others. But this in itself had a certain appeal, and Toomey's desire for her was increased at seeing her try to maintain her poise as she dealt with concepts that seemed difficult for her to understand. Even Toomey found the subject easier than she did.

The project assigned to them by the young professor was to measure the comparative sex drive of the male and female white rat by means of placing an electric grid between them and determining which—the male or the female—would undergo the greater amount of electric shock in order to reach the other.

This was not an experiment that was sexually arousing. Quite the opposite, actually, since it associated the mating instinct with pain. Moreover, the statistics they came up with tended to indicate that the female would tolerate a larger amount of punishment in order to get to the male than the male would withstand in order to get to the female. Which was not the way Toomey thought it should be. He would have preferred that the statistics prove conclusively that the male white rat would undergo even the most excruciating agony in order to get to the female so that that beautiful and beloved creature would not have to hurt her tender feet or inconvenience herself in any way in order to find bliss and fulfillment.

But, despite the handicap imposed by the association between sex and blistered feet, romance flowered, and in the spring, when they were writing up their tentative conclusions, they more or less mutually agreed that they should get married.

So they did. In a small and quiet ceremony that summer in Baldwinsville.

There were many practical advantages to their being married. They saved money by living together, and they were able to help each other with their work. Toomey switched from a major in physical education to majoring in psychology and they began making plans for their future. She was honest enough to admit that she would not be able to make it through medical school, so she could not become a psychiatrist. But she could get a Ph.D. in psychology and be qualified as an analyst in her father's clinic. Which was what she wanted more than anything else, anyway. And Toomey said that he didn't want to go to medical school either, and if working as an analyst in her father's clinic was what she wanted, then that was what he wanted, too.

(Early in their relationship, Gertrude had told Toomey that Indiana University had not been her first choice. She had applied at three eastern universities and had been turned down.

Later, she told him that he, too, had not been her first choice. Her first choice had been the young professor. She had loved him and had, in fact, had a brief affair with him. His pairing her with Toomey had been a cruel joke on his part.

Much later, toward the end of their marriage, she gave him the ultimate insult. She told him bluntly, "And I wouldn't even want you as my therapist!")

After graduation he continued in school and she went to work to help pay his way. And she saw to it that he kept at his studies until he had finally reached that point where the patients at Creighton called him Doctor Bougereau and would lie down on the couch and tell him what was bothering them. Then she reminded him that she had worked to get him through school and expected him to do the same for her. He said, "Of course." That had been the understanding. Like two people getting to the top of the wall. She helps him to the top, then he gives her a hand up. A good and decent arrangement. The way that they had always planned it.

So she, too, after a while, got her degree and the patients at Creighton called her Doctor Bougereau and talked to her about their problems. And why they were unhappy.

About this time Toomey mentioned something else that he thought had been part of the understanding between them.

That someday they'd have a family. A couple kids, anyway. He'd looked forward to that.

"One of us," he said jokingly, "should have a baby. And I don't think I can."

She said, "I can't either. My father is counting on me to take over for him after he retires. Besides, when you have patients dependent upon you and needing to see you every day, you can't take nine months out to have a baby."

"It doesn't take nine months," he said.

She said, "Yes it does."

Shortly after that, Toomey told her that he was now tired of Creighton Medical Center and that he thought he'd be moving along.

"Too many Doctor Bougereaus," he said, "will drive these patients crazy."

She said, "All right."

The divorce was amicable. No hard feelings. No problems. Everything was divided evenly. Property, money, things like books.

She had first choice. She took the six-volume collected works of Sigmund Freud. He took the illustrated hardcover *Freshwater Fishing in America.*

And so it went.

At the end she told him that she was sorry she had not been able to really love him. Though she had tried.

He said he understood.

He left Creighton Medical Center and joined the staff of the Wakefield County Industrial School for boys. Delinquent and predelinquent boys from age ten to seventeen, referred by the courts or state agencies. They were tough kids and had little motivation toward trying to understand more about themselves and why they were doing what they were doing. But it was an interesting challenge. And although it kept him busy, he still found time to set up an office in town and have private patients evenings and Saturdays.

In what little spare time he had, which was not much, he did a bit of serious thinking and a little casual drinking.

Actually, as Toomey told himself much later, it should have been the other way around.

If his thinking had been less serious he probably would never have become involved with Janet Spengler, who was chairman of a committee organized by the parent-teacher association to study ways to deal with disciplinary problems in the public schools. She had heard about him, went to see him, and talked him into serving as a free consultant to her group.

And if his drinking had been less casual and more serious, he reminded himself, they would probably not have met in the first place, because she didn't drink.

Anyway, he attended one of the meetings of her committee and gave her a ride home afterwards. She lived, he was surprised to find, in one of the poorer sections of town. And was having a hard time getting by financially.

It so happened that that was the night of the day that her divorce had become final. After ten long years of marriage. Ten hard years characterized by violent quarrels, stormy separations, and tearful reconciliations. Ten years of stress and strain that had left her and her four beautiful children tense and exhausted.

Her husband had not been a good provider, had quit a job anytime he felt like it whether he had another one to go to or not, had beat her and the kids, had left for days at a time, once for two weeks. It never seemed to bother him whether there was food in the house or not.

She told him all about it. And he listened. Was sympathetic and understanding. And he said he could understand how happy she must feel to be finally free from such an unsatisfactory relationship.

But when she asked him if he could guess what she'd like to do now, now that she was free at last, he said, "No. What?"

She said she wanted to make love again to a man, once again as a free woman.

He could understand that, too. So he stayed.

She was attractive, sensual, down to earth, liked cookouts, picnics, television, and sex.

The children ranged from three to nine. Two boys and two

girls. Three, five, seven, and nine years old.

He romped with them on the living-room rug, played games with them in the park, took them for walks in the woods, taught them to catch sunfish from the shore at Lake Lashmore. And their happy cries of welcome when he came to visit were a delight to his ears.

As Janet put it, for a long time they'd needed a man around the house. "And," she added, "so have I."

And smiled at him. And said that he'd make her and the children very happy if he'd stay with them permanently.

What the hell! Why not?

He said, "Sure." And they laughed, put the kids to bed, watched TV for a while, then, after they were sure the kids were all asleep, took a blanket outside and made love in the moonlight.

And for a while it was good. A loving wife to come home to, to please and be pleased by, and four kids to enjoy. Enough to make a hard day's work seem worth while.

And birthdays. With four kids and a wife it seemed that it was almost always someone's birthday.

Her former husband visited, of course. He was, after all, the kids' father. And he, too, was allowed to romp with them on the rug and play with them in the park and sit by the edge of the lake and watch them catch sunfish. And send them presents and sometimes take them out to Burger Heaven for dinner.

Because he usually wasn't working, he visited quite often. Made himself at home. He would have welcomed an invitation to stay overnight. Wasn't easy to get rid of.

He asked Janet to keep him informed of the children's problems at home and at school. As their father, he was concerned about them. And once when the older boy got into a fight during gym class and was suspended from school for three days, he went down and complained to the principal about it.

She told him that she thought a lot of the kids' problems were caused by the tensions resulting from their being torn between their real father and their stepfather. And she said she could understand how they felt. She said that sometimes she felt the same way.

After all, she told him, after you've lived with a man ten

years and shared the trials and tribulations of raising four kids, you can't forget that person overnight.

That, he told her, was the way he felt, too.

Toomey suggested to her that maybe it would be better if she made a definite choice between him and the children's real father and she said she'd been asking herself that same question. She didn't know what to think. It was such a hard decision.

She said that she would have to have a conference with the children to see how they felt.

Before they separated, he outfitted the kids with new clothes, bought her a few things he knew she needed, agreed that she could say in court that he'd been cruel and inhuman and drank too much.

She thanked him for being so generous.

"That's all right."

She said, "You're a nice person. I'm sorry that I was never able to love you as much as I should have."

He said that he understood.

After she had gone back to her former husband, Toomey quit his job, closed up his office, and paid his bills. And did a little serious drinking.

He was thirty-seven years old. Two weeks short of being thirty-eight.

He shook his head, looked at his reflection in the mirror, and laughed.

And ordered one last bourbon on the rocks.

One Thursday morning in early December, Toomey got into his car and headed north into Massachusetts, then east on Route 90. He was headed for Cape Cod. It would be quiet there this time of year. The weather was still warm and he could walk along the beach and look at the ocean and watch the clouds and the birds and maybe even check out the fishing.

He didn't get even as far as Worcester.

Toomey had an experience on the turnpike that shook him up as much as anything he had ever experienced before. More, even.

Afterwards, he turned around and headed back west. To

Munsen. There he stopped at a place called Harvey's Variety Store, had a cup of coffee at their little luncheonette, bought some cigars, and got into a long conversation with the proprietor.

Toomey said that he planned to stay in Munsen for a while. Didn't say for how long or why, just that that was what he had decided to do.

That sounded sensible, Harvey said. And told him that he had something that might interest him.

What Harvey had was a building to rent. An old couple had been running a gift shop there for years, but they were retiring at the end of this month and were going to move to Florida. In their gift shop they featured woven baskets that they made themselves. And, according to Harvey, they had made a good living at it.

Harvey even had a small cottage about fifty yards from the shop that he'd be willing to rent. That, too, would be vacant when the old couple moved out. Two bedrooms, partly furnished. Comfortable. And the property went all the way down to the lake. Where there was a dock and a rowboat. The boat was pulled up on shore now, of course, for the winter. But he could go take a look at it if he wanted to. The boat and the dock went with the property.

The owners of the Munsen Roadside Gift Shop, Mr. and Mrs. Charles Crandall, showed him how easy it was to make baskets. Some of the very complicated ones that Mrs. Crandall made as special items took a lot of time and didn't bring as much profit, but the smaller ones were easy to make and during the summer sold as fast as you could make them. And the ones that were used to hold pots for hanging house plants could be sold by the hundreds, if you had them.

They told him about a Mrs. Murphey, Mary Murphey, a widow, who had been with them for years and who knew all about the business and the weaving of baskets. A good worker, efficient, very reliable. They said that she probably would be happy to work for him if he decided to take over the business.

32

Harvey reported that people came from miles around because the bass fishing here was so good. Especially from a rowboat about sunrise, when the lake is smooth as glass and the air fresh and clean. Or on a quiet summer evening, about the time the sun is setting behind those beautiful hills, and everything is calm and peaceful.

Try, Harvey suggested, along the lily pads about thirty or forty yards south of the dock.

That's where the big ones are.

Toomey didn't run the place as a gift shop. He closed that down. Instead, he concentrated on making only the small and simple baskets that were currently in vogue and sold them in large quantities to a wholesaler in Boston. And changed the name of the place to Baskets and Baskets.

Some members of the community weren't too happy about that. They thought a gift shop was better for the tourist business. And because the new owner seemed to concentrate on getting sexy-looking young women to work for him, they wondered just what was going on.

The question was raised as to whether he now ran a manufacturing business rather than a store. Which would not be in conformity with zoning regulations. And by spring, people were talking about whether maybe something should be done.

5

On Thanksgiving Day of the thirty-second year of her life, Toni Heller made one of the biggest decisions of her lifetime. Not hurriedly or capriciously, but after thinking about it carefully all day long.

What she decided was what it was she wanted for Christmas.

That is not ordinarily a very big or important decision. But in this case it was something rather special. It was not something mundane, like a new set of mechanic's tools, luggage, a vacation trip to some exotic spot, or a new washing machine. It was something much more imaginative. Something she could expect to enjoy for the rest of her life.

The first person to hear about it was a woman named Maxine Folger, one of the people she shared the house with. Maxine had been living there for nearly two months. She was twenty-one years old and had dropped out of college because she had realized that she didn't know what she really wanted to study and she didn't want her parents to waste any more money. She would return, she had promised, after she had a better idea of what she wanted out of college. In the meantime, she was driving a school bus, taking flute lessons and yoga instruction, and doing some volunteer work at the Women's Center in Northampton.

At first she seemed not sure that she had heard correctly, and asked Toni to repeat it. Which Toni did. And for a moment they both were silent.

Then Maxine said, "Toni! That is so *beautiful*."

Toni said, "It's what I want, I know. I've been thinking about it all day."

They were sitting in front of the fireplace finishing a bottle of Lambrusco left from the Thanksgiving dinner. Toni's little girl was asleep and the two other women who lived in the house had gone out.

"Do you think you can really go through with it?"

Toni said that of course she could. "Because it's what I want. I know that."

She said, "I've been making my own decisions for as long as I can remember. Sometimes right, sometimes wrong. And now I'm old enough to know when I'm making one that's right."

She added, after a moment, "That's the one thing more I need to make me happy."

Maxine shook her head in admiration. "That is so beautiful, Toni."

She said, "You are such a great person. I admire you so much."

And for a while they looked silently into the fire and watched the bits of flame leap and dart from one spot to another.

"I admire people who know what they really want," Maxine said. "I wish I did."

It is true that Toni had been making her own decisions for a long time, starting with a small but significant decision she had been asked to make when she was only seven years old. That was when her mother told her that she would leave it up to her to decide whether she wanted her friends to call her Anne or Toni.

No one, of course, called her Antoinette. Not even her mother, who in some stubborn and reckless moment had insisted that her daughter be named Antoinette Marie so that her French side of the family would not be entirely swallowed up by the Irish family she had married into.

(Michael, Patrick, and Sean were all right for the boys, but the girl, by God, was going to be named Antoinette.)

A few people were calling her Anne, but mostly school teachers and girls who wore party dresses. But her brothers had been calling her Toni for years.

So that decision was an easy one.

It was Toni at age seven and still Toni now that she was thirty-two.

Sometimes people asked her how come a woman turns out to be an automobile mechanic. She always told them that if a woman wants to be an automobile mechanic, then she can get to be an automobile mechanic. Women get to be what they want, same as men.

But what people usually meant was how could a woman get to be an automobile mechanic after they've decided that that is what they want to be. And then she would admit that if you have an uncle who owns a garage, that helps.

It also helps, she said, if you are a little too tall to look good in the cute kind of outfits cocktail waitresses have to wear. And if you aren't good looking enough so that businessmen offer you large sums of money to be a receptionist. And if you don't like working in an office, anyway.

She wasn't married.

She had been, though. When she was twenty. Married to a tall, good-looking young man with long blond hair, a weak nature, a father who was a doctor, and an easy access to drugs.

His name was Mark Heller. He had been her age, and they had met while they were both attending Farmington Community College. He had been using and selling drugs since his second year of high school. Periodically he would be arrested, placed on probation, and given some form of rehabilitation plan acceptable to the judge. The requirement that he attend Farmington Community College was part of his current rehabilitation program. He was trying very hard, he said, to succeed in school and not violate his probation. He was afraid of what would happen if he had to go back to court again.

She had not been attracted to him at first, and had turned down a number of invitations. He was not her type. He came from the wealthy class. The country-club set. The kind of people she had never felt comfortable with.

But he had persisted, and looked hurt when she refused to go out with him. He asked why, and that made her think about it.

The only answer she could give herself was that she was prejudiced against the class of people he came from.

Which amused her. And she had to laugh at the recognition that she, who had been raised to believe that it was wrong to be prejudiced against any kind of people, was herself acting in a very prejudiced way.

So she went out with him. To the movies a time or two. To a concert once.

Then it was early June and he took her sailing on Lake Mahaiwe, then swimming at the country club. Drinks by the side of the pool. Then dinner. And it was all rather nice.

One could, she told a friend, become addicted rather easily to that kind of thing.

Looking back on it, she was embarrassed to recall how easily she had become comfortable with the kind of people her father had always railed against. The moneyed crowd, as he had called them. The doctors, lawyers, bankers, corporation executives, and big property owners. And their families.

They had accepted her more easily than she had accepted them.

And all of them thought she was wonderful.

She was the opposite of Mark in almost every way. He was weak and irresponsible, she was strong and stable. He didn't really want to be in college, she loved it. He was egocentric and self-indulgent, whereas she was kind, considerate, and, above all, sympathetic. She was, in fact, just what he needed.

That was what his parents told her. She could be his salvation, they said. They told her she was beautiful, charming, intelligent, and a lady. Just right for Mark. Who was actually brilliant, they said. He just happened to be going through a troubled period.

And when you are only twenty years old you can believe things like that.

The tennis pro gave Mark and her lessons. His parents gave her clothes, gifts, flattery. And, understandably, her head spun a little.

She could do it. She could make him into a different kind of person. It would be a great achievement on her part and a most humanitarian thing to do.

And they did, after all, have good times together. And all her girl friends envied her. And her brothers had stopped kidding her about being part of the country-club set. The two oldest were now making enough money that they could probably have joined the country club themselves if they wanted to.

They were married in early September. Just in time for a short honeymoon before returning to school. They settled down in a small one-bedroom apartment on the west side and lived on his allowance from his father, plus a little extra that she made working part time in the college library.

Everything was going well and life was enjoyable.

On the campus, people knew and liked them both. And on the tennis court, as a doubles team, they played almost flawlessly.

In her philosophy and social studies classes she was outstanding.

In the bathroom he was shooting up.

In February he almost died of an overdose. And was out of the hospital less than a week when he was arrested for selling drugs to a sixteen-year-old boy.

Later, feeling bad and berating herself for not having been aware of what was really happening, she admitted to his parents that she supposed she had somehow failed. And they said that they supposed so, too. And she woke up.

She got a divorce, left school, and went to live with her aunt and uncle in Coultraine and got a job clerking in a bookstore.

That was fun, and for a while she was happy once more.

She took off for Vermont in the summer with Carl, who was strong, lean, broad shouldered. A self-sufficient man seeking the good life. He made a living doing whatever kind of work the wealthy people in the Bennington area needed to have done. He was woodsman, carpenter, mason, guard, and caretaker of estates belonging to the rich, who wintered in the South. Living quarters were always provided.

Those were good years. There was a lot to learn, books to read, small skills to develop, interesting people her own age to get to know, new ideas to explore. And no pressure to conform or to do anything that you don't want to do.

They were always living in other people's property, though, with little that was their own, and that bothered her a bit. It did not quite fit with her idea of independence.

But there was fun and love and great parties in the meadows in the summertime, with enough blue sky and wild flowers for everyone. Nude swimming, usually in some abandoned quarry off a back country road. And cross-country skiing in the winter, with fireplaces afterwards, and hot spiced cider and guitar music.

Once she mentioned that someday she'd like to get married and have children. Carl said that he didn't plan to do either.

After a while she found herself a job in Bennington and took a course in modern romantic poetry at the college at night. The instructor liked her work. He liked her, too. He was young, tall, thin, with blond hair. Delicate, in a way. Admired Dylan Thomas, hated women poets. Had once visited Auden.

With him she got an intensity of feeling that she had not known before. She lived with him in April and May in that early summer of her life. And it was good.

After school was out, he took a six-week trip west and didn't take her with him. And when he came back she broke the news to him that she was pregnant. The look on his face was one that she would never forget. Utter dismay. His life was ruined! And he hit the flat of his hand against the side of his head dramatically and said that he hoped to God she wasn't going to tell him that the child was his.

She lied to him and said of course not. And he believed her.

Back in Coultraine, she had the baby, moved into a big house and shared expenses with three other women, and, as soon as she felt well enough, started helping out her Uncle Mike at the garage. Started learning to work on cars. Small jobs at first, then bigger ones.

She had now been there three years. According to Mike, she was as good as any other mechanic in the shop. Maybe better.

So things weren't too bad. Her girl was beautiful, happy, and getting a lot of good care. And that's important.

There were men in her life, of course, but only for short periods, usually.

There had been an insurance salesman with whom she'd gone out a few times. But he had seemed to be embarrassed by the fact that she was an automobile mechanic and didn't try to conceal it. He had subtly talked to her about maybe finding some other kind of work more befitting the fact that she was a woman. Which she found amusing. When she told him that she wouldn't be able to go out with him anymore, she said it was because she was going to get a job driving a taxi nights.

Then there had been a young pharmacist, a year younger than she, whom she'd gone out with for six months or more. He had never been married, lived alone in an apartment in the middle of town, had never been outside the state of Massachusetts, and spent much of his time caring for an elderly mother in North Cummington. A good person, and she had liked him. He had been very inexperienced in certain areas, and she had helped him. He had helped her, too, by being so devoted and by saying the kinds of things that every once in a while a woman needs to hear a man say. And when she had to tell him that she didn't really want to accept his offer of marriage, it was not easy to explain why.

And for a while she didn't go out with anyone.

As is true with most people, there still persisted in her mind the belief that there was a certain person she would someday meet who was just right. Someone she'd meet at a party or at work or at a gathering of some kind. It was not likely that he would be a college professor or a movie director or a famous writer, but he'd be intelligent and capable in some field of work. And they'd talk a bit and he'd suggest they go swimming Sunday or boating or on a picnic. Or something.

But no. *First*, he'd ask if she was married, and she'd say no. And you would be able to tell by the light in his eyes that he was glad to hear that.

Then he'd ask if he could see her the next day and she'd say

41

yes. She'd like that. But she'd say that she'd want to bring her little girl along. And his eyes would light up even more.

"You have a child?"

"Yes."

He'd say, "Hey, that's nice!"

A nice fantasy, but nothing like that ever happened.

Toni had now reached the advanced age of thirty-two, which is not many years short of the halfway mark. Time to accept reluctantly the fact that she wasn't going to end up with the kind of family life she'd once been led to expect. Although there would no doubt always be men in her life, there wasn't going to be that suburban house, a handsome and loving husband, two children, a late-model station wagon, and a dog. Maybe a swimming pool.

Sometimes she looked in the mirror, at the face that was a little too long, teeth that got more attention than was necessary, skin that looked more weatherbeaten than the ones you see on the facial-cream commercials on TV, and work-roughened hands, and thought that maybe it was time to close out the romantic hopes.

The last three men she'd gone out with had been salesmen, two who weren't making any money and were about to quit, and one who was trying to conceal the fact that he was married.

Then came the Thanksgiving of her thirty-second year. It had been a happy day at the house, friends in for dinner, good holiday spirit. And now the dishes were done, her girl in bed, the guests had gone, as were two of the other women who lived in the house, and she was sitting in front of the fireplace with Maxine.

It was quiet and peaceful. There was soft music from the FM radio. For a long while the two of them had been sitting there silently watching the fire.

Toni said, "I decided today that there is one more thing I want. And I'm going to give it to myself for Christmas."

Maxine said, "What's that?"

Toni said, "I want another child."

She took the bottle of Lambrusco and carefully divided it equally between Maxine and herself.

She said, "I want to wake up Christmas morning knowing that I have a child growing inside me. And that's going to be my Christmas present to myself."

Maxine's reaction was admiration of the strongest and deepest kind. She sat up, reached out and touched Toni's arm. "Toni! That's so *beautiful!*"

She shook her head, as if the whole thing was almost more than she could deal with. She said, "You're so goddam great. I admire you so much."

She almost had tears in her eyes.

"I'm going to pick out a man to get pregnant by," Toni said. "Someone I don't know. Someone I'll never see again."

For a moment they sipped their wine in silence and looked into the fire.

"I want him to be intelligent, of course. Tall, I think, and reasonably good looking."

After a moment, she said, "Healthy. And from a healthy family."

Another moment, and she added, "Sensitive and kind. If that's not asking too much."

A sip of wine, then she said, "I want to raise it as my own child. I don't want the father to know that somewhere there is a child of his. And I don't want to know who or where the father is."

Toni said, "That way, I won't be tempted in some weak moment to try to find him."

"That is so goddam beautiful!"

Toni had already made the necessary calculations. She should find her man about seven or eight days from now, and let him make love to her.

If she did, she'd be able to wake up on Christmas morning, rub her hand across her stomach, and smile happily.

This is what she'd say:

"Merry Christmas, Toni!"

She said to Maxine, "It would be nice if it were a boy this

time. Myra needs a little brother."

"It will be," Maxine said. "I know it will."

"What I have to do now," Toni said, "is figure out how to find the kind of man I'm looking for."

"You can do that easily. I'm sure you can."

Toni said, "I don't know. I'm not so certain."

6

Mrs. Murphey came into the office at four o'clock to say that the girls were asking if they could leave early.

As she waited for his answer, she volunteered the information that actually it was pretty hot out there. Even with all the windows open.

"According to the radio, the official temperature is ninety-four degrees."

Toomey said, "Of course they can leave early. I should have thought of that myself."

"I think they want to go swimming."

Toomey said he thought that sounded sensible.

"Tell them I said that when they sign out to put down five o'clock."

She shook her head at that last part. She didn't see how he could expect to stay in business if he paid the workers for more hours than they actually worked.

"Why don't you leave early yourself? It's as hot out there for you as it is for them."

Mrs. Murphey said that she didn't really mind the heat. But if the others were leaving, she would, too. She was going up to Farmington for dinner tonight at her son's house. Michael. The dentist. He'd only recently had a swimming pool installed in his backyard. She wanted to try it out.

"But while I'm here," she said, "I've got a couple things I need to talk to you about."

She amended that. "Three things."

"All right." And he took some papers off the chair by the desk so she could sit down.

Mrs. Murphey was a tall, angular woman. Unsmiling, mostly, but not for the lack of a sense of humor or because she thought life was hard. Her serious expression was a long-time habit, not an indication of her state of being. Perhaps a family characteristic. Something she had copied from her mother, maybe. Or her father. Maybe he had been a poker player.

Her husband had been a worker at the New England Electric Company and a strong union man. A shop steward. He had drowned fifteen years ago in a boating accident on Lake George while on a fishing trip with some friends from the factory. She had three sons and a daughter, and although she didn't talk about them much, from what she did say you could tell that she approved of all of them.

Two sons, one a lawyer and one a dentist, lived in Farmington. Both had gone south in the early sixties to work for the voter-registration program for blacks. The third son, her youngest, lived in Boston and was a social worker for the State Department of Public Welfare. He was the only one of the three who was not married. He came home to visit about once a month.

Her daughter, Myra's mother, lived in Coultraine. She didn't talk about her daughter very much. Once she mentioned that Myra's mother was pregnant, and she seemed to be happy about that.

Another grandchild, that would be nice.

"First," she said, "Glenna is testing me to see how far she can go before I have to ask you to fire her."

Toomey nodded. "That's too bad. I'm sorry."

He said, "She's one of the girls I hired, isn't she?"

Mrs. Murphey smiled a little. "Yes, she is."

This was part of a small joke they had between them. Which of them hired the girls who worked out best, and which hired the ones who caused trouble.

On days when Toomey was in Boston, if they were shorthanded and there was someone who wanted to start working, she was authorized to put them on the payroll. And her choices always seemed to work out well. He had, in fact, admitted more than once that her judgment seemed to be better than his.

Of the four girls working now, she had hired two and he had hired two. Hers were not only good workers, but helped to make the shop a pleasant place to work.

"Remember, though," Toomey said, "I hired her because I was asked to do so as a favor to someone."

She shrugged her shoulders slightly to show that that was more or less irrelevant, as far as she could see.

"Anyway, I wish you'd talk to her. Tell her she's got to quit trying to make me angry. And that she's got to do more work."

He asked her what Glenna did that made her angry, and Mrs. Murphey provided a rather long list of things that Glenna had discovered could annoy her. All of them were directly and personally insulting. Mocking her, making fun of her clothes, calling her names. That kind of thing.

Toomey said he didn't like the idea of firing anyone, but he'd see that she either changed her attitude or found a job somewhere else.

"I'll call her into the office tomorrow," Toomey promised. "I've got to talk to her anyway about her friends and their motorcycles."

Glenna was eighteen years old, an angry, rebellious girl who had been working at Baskets and Baskets for about a month. Toomey had hired her at the request of a social worker from Farmington who had worked with Glenna when she was a foster child. She had come from a difficult home situation to which she had returned when she was eighteen, three months ago. She had a boyfriend, about twenty-five years old, who rode with a motorcycle group called the Hornets. Lately her boyfriend had been picking her up after work, usually accompanied by two or three of his friends. They parked in front of the building while they waited, kept the motors of the bikes running, revving them up every once in a while. Which was bad enough, but when Glenna did finally come out and everyone gunned his motor at the same time it was like a Boeing 707 heading down the runway and picking up speed.

Mrs. Boughton, across the street, who was elderly and whose nerves and patience weren't as good as they once had been, had complained to the police.

"Nicocci said that Mrs. Boughton called him about it," Toomey said.

"Good." Mrs. Murphey said that he should do something about it.

"It's probably my responsibility," Toomey said. "So I'll do something about it. And I'll see that Glenna stops giving you trouble."

Okay. So much for that.

"What else?"

"Angela."

She was the other girl he had hired.

"What about Angela?"

"She's about to drive all of us crazy. She's always telling everyone how sick they are. That we're all neurotic. How we should all of us be in mental hospitals. And she does only half as much work as the others, with the possible exception of Glenna."

"Just a minute," Toomey said. "You must remember that I hired her because the Reverend Osterman asked me to."

She raised her eyebrows a little. So?

"If she had just walked in off the street looking for a job," Toomey said, "you can be sure that I would never have hired her."

He said, "I know enough about people to know that she would only cause trouble."

She didn't disagree, but neither did she nod her head to show that she was certain he was right.

He was impressed again with what a perfect poker face she had. He would hate to have to sit across the table from her some

48

night and watch her push her whole pile of chips into the center of the table and then have to try to figure out if she was bluffing or not.

"Someday," he said, "I'm going to let you do all the hiring. I think then that things will be better."

She nodded, almost imperceptibly, but enough to show that she agreed.

"Anyway," he said, "Getting back to Angela. She has, as you know, been in and out of mental hospitals during the last seven or eight years."

Mrs. Murphey knew that, of course. Most of the conversation in the shop was based on what the workers had or hadn't done during their lives up to this point. And what they wanted to do from now on.

"Reverend Osterman, in Farmington, has been counseling Angela for the last few months. Since she came back from New Mexico. He thought it would be good therapy for her to try to hold down a regular job."

That was something she could agree with. She nodded several times to indicate her approval.

She said, "It should be easy for him to find her some kind of job around the church."

It *was* hot. Toomey took a handkerchief from his pocket and touched it to his forehead.

"She keeps telling me," Mrs. Murphey said, "that I'm trying to drive her to commit suicide. And that if she *does* commit suicide, it will all be my fault."

Toomey opened the collar of his shirt a bit more. And wondered if it would be cool enough to go out in the boat. Decided it would be. Right after work. He would take a half dozen cans of beer and fish on the shady side of the lake. Whether there were any fish there or not.

"I'm sorry the girls give you such a hard time," Toomey said. "You're very patient with them."

The compliment seemed to please her.

"They would drive me out of my mind," Toomey said. "Except for Helen and Yolanda, that is. They are great kids and I've become very fond of them."

Those were the two she had hired.

49

"I'll talk to Angela," Toomey said. "I'll talk to her and Glenna tomorrow."

"Thank you."

"If she does commit suicide," Toomey said, "and she might, believe me, it will be no fault of yours. You can be sure of that."

She seemed satisfied with that. So he asked her, "What's the third thing?"

The third thing was that Myra's mother might have to ask her to keep Myra another couple of weeks more. Unless she was too much of a burden on Toomey. Her being around the shop so much and in his office most of the time.

"The day-care center is closing down for two weeks so the staff can have a little vacation. So it would help if the girl could stay with me a little longer."

Toomey told her he was glad to hear that. He enjoyed having the child around.

"I remember once you said your daughter was pregnant."

"She is. But she still works part time because she needs the money."

Toomey asked when the baby was due, and she said early in September.

Although Mrs. Murphey had never said that her daughter wasn't married, Toomey had by now concluded that she was either single or divorced. If there was a husband, some mention of him would have come into the conversation by now.

Toomey said that she sounded like a great person and that he'd like to meet her sometime.

"She'd like to meet you," Mrs. Murphey said. "She's heard Myra talk so much about you."

That pleased him. He asked if there was anything else that she wanted to mention and she said there wasn't. He suggested again that she, too, leave early. She said she probably would.

"And put down five o'clock. It fouls up my records when anyone puts down anything other than five o'clock."

She agreed, reluctantly, and left to tell the girls that they could leave anytime they wanted to.

Toomey helped Myra put the crayons and things away. They put the toys back in the box and stacked the coloring books again in the corner. He told her that he hoped she would be able to come back and visit with him again tomorrow, and apparently she would be able to work that into her schedule because she said she'd be back.

A moment later one of the girls came to Toomey's office to tell him that everyone said thanks for letting them off early.

This was Yolanda. She was twenty years old and had been working at Baskets and Baskets since the middle of June. She was blond, slender, with blue eyes and a laughing face. She had finished one year of college and was going back in the fall. She was barefoot, wearing ragged and patched blue jeans that didn't come up too high on the hips, and a thin yellow shirt with the top open and the bottom part rolled up and tied just below her breasts.

"Everyone said to ask you if you wanted to come with us. We're going to the old quarry."

She stood there smiling invitingly, young and open and honest and really meaning it that they would be happy to have him join them. She tossed her long blond hair back and waited for his answer. Long legs, bare midriff, and browned breasts pushing out around the tightly tied thin yellow shirt. And anyone with even a modicum of imagination could visualize how very beautiful it would be at the old quarry about twenty minutes from now.

He said, "Thanks, Yolanda. But I think not. And I do appreciate your asking me."

"If you don't feel like swimming," she said, "you could just come along and watch. Or bring your fishing pole. There's fish there. I've seen them."

Again he said, "Thanks, Yolanda. It's really nice of you to suggest it. But I promised Roman I'd take him for a swim down at the lake. There's a muskrat down there he's been trying for weeks to catch. He thinks maybe tonight he can do it."

She laughed at that and moved over to where Roman was lying and rubbed his head and stroked his back.

Roman thumped his tail happily for a moment or two, then moved his head a bit and started licking her on the foot and ankle.

Toomey said, "Stop it, Roman."

But Yolanda said, "That's all right. I don't mind. It kind of tickles." And she rubbed his stomach and scratched behind his ears some more.

After what seemed like a long while, she finally headed for the door.

Toomey said, "Have a good swim." And she said thanks.

"You have a good time fishing."

"Thanks."

He called Lorraine's number. And told her he wanted to come over tonight.

"I need to go to bed with you."

She asked how come. "You were here only last night."

Toomey said he supposed that it was the hot weather. Maybe the humidity.

She said, "All right. You talked me into it. But make it late. About ten o'clock. Kate and I are going to a movie."

He complained about that. "Ten o'clock is a long time from now."

"Not too long," she said. "You can wait five hours."

"Besides," Toomey said, "I think Kate should stay home with her kids for a change."

Lorraine said that Kate deserved a night out. "And it won't hurt you to wait. That will only make it all the more enjoyable."

Before she hung up she said, "You sound as if you'd had a hard day."

He said, "No more than usual. It's just that it's so very hot in here."

"That's your own fault," she said. "From what I hear, you let the kids run around with practically no clothes on."

He told her he'd see her at ten o'clock. And they both said good-bye and hung up.

Lorraine LeClair lived in Hartsdale, which is halfway between Munsen and Farmington. It is a residential area of high-income families. Large houses on beautifully landscaped lots. Private swimming pools. That sort of thing.

Lorraine lived in one such home. An eight-room house, flagstone patio, swimming pool, two-car garage, two and three-fourths acres. She had two teen-age children and a former husband that she'd ordered out of the house a year ago. That was the night she had intentionally come home from her mother's a day early because she had suspected that he was having an affair with another woman. And had found him in bed with his new love, a slender and blond young man whom she recognized as a lifeguard from the country club the summer before.

She had screamed at them, "Get out! Out! Before I call the police. Both of you!"

She did in fact move toward the phone to emphasize the point.

When he said that he didn't have a place to go she told him that she didn't care. He could spend the night at the YMCA as far as she was concerned.

Which, she later found out, was like ordering a surfer to Hawaii. Or arbitrarily transferring a skier to a job in Vermont for the winter.

Anyway, he had gone. Leaving her angry, embarrassed, and frustrated.

And, after a while, lonely.

Her friend, Kate Dawson, who lived in Munsen, told her some interesting things about the new man in town, so she went down to his place of business one afternoon to check him out.

He looked all right. Nothing special, but all right. Big, though. And she liked big men.

She asked him if he'd make her a special basket for her laundry room, round and three feet high, like the one she'd seen in *House Beautiful*. She had brought with her a picture from the magazine and showed that to him.

At first he said that they didn't make special orders, but she was wearing the gray slacks and the beige sweater from Bonwit Teller in New York City. And she saw that he noticed. She asked, with that ingratiating little smile that she had, if he'd make her one as a special favor and drop it off at her house that night. Or the next.

He finally agreed to do it. And did. And dropped it off at her house the next night. And at first she thought that he was actually going to just take the money she gave him and leave. But this time she was wearing the casual red evening gown, also from Bonwit Teller. And when she asked if he'd like a drink before he left, he said that he would try one.

"What would you like?"

He didn't seem to care. Anything would do, he said. "Anything you have is all right. Beer, wine, or just an ordinary little whiskey or bourbon would be fine."

She paused part way to the liquor cabinet, slowly turned and smiled at him reprovingly. She gave him the kind of look that gently but firmly makes it clear that one doesn't come into a room of this kind, a room decorated with the most exquisite taste, with expensive furnishings, art, elegance, and style, and ask for an ordinary little whiskey.

Not even people who weave baskets for a living.

"I make it a point, Mr. Bougereau"—and here she pulled her lips together in a certain way she had—"never to have in my house anything that is just ordinary."

Her eyes scolded him. But nicely. "Would Jack Daniels do?"

He said that that would be all right.

She said that she would fix him a drink and suggested he make himself comfortable. Which he did.

He tossed his jacket on the couch, sat down in the best chair, and without asking whether or not it was all right, lit a cigar.

She found him to be a good lover. And until that night some months later when she got very angry with him and yelled at him to get out and stay out, he filled most enjoyably that part of her life that required a man.

He was not the most passionate lover she had ever known, offered no poetic thoughts or sentimental words, no protestations of love. Sometimes he even seemed distracted by other thoughts or memories. She even asked him once if he had another lover, and he said that he guessed he hadn't.

He never left her unsatisfied. He was very thorough. Very professional. Like a competent football team slowly grinding out yardage, bit by bit. Pushing you happily back toward your own goal line.

She once told her friend, Kate, what it was like when Toomey reached orgasm. She first described it as being something like an earthquake. But she changed that to say that it was more like maybe a big pickup truck that's been idling at a high rate, then the ignition is turned off and for several seconds there is a sort of shaking, shuddering, and vibrating and rocking back and forth. And then the whole thing sort of collapses.

The night she told Kate about it they both laughed so hard that they almost collapsed themselves.

"It's like all four wheels slowly give way," Lorraine said, "and the whole thing gradually settles down on you!"

And they held each other and laughed so hard they almost got hysterical.

Lorraine found herself becoming fond of Toomey. He was not bad looking, in a way, was considerate and understanding. And the children liked him, too.

Her fifteen-year-old son, Greg, liked to talk with Toomey about sports, especially football. He seemed to know a lot about the game.

She asked him once if he'd played football in high school and he said yes, he had played some.

Her thirteen-year-old girl, Melanie, didn't talk with Toomey much, but she didn't seem to mind his being around. Which was pretty good. If any other adult came to the house she went flying up to her room.

But although she liked him and was glad to have him around, she knew that she didn't really love him. And once she told him so.

It was late one night. They were in bed and had just finished making love. She was lying there with her head on his shoulder and her hand on his chest, when she suddenly felt a small surge of affection for this nice beast of a man who lay there breathing so heavily, his eyes closed, his arm beneath her head and his heavy hand gently on her shoulder.

He was like a big, unsophisticated country boy. Simple, but

with a certain kind of crude charm that she had to admit appealed to her.

She moved her head enough to kiss him softly on the chest. And let her hand run affectionately down his body, ending with a firm pat on his thigh.

"Toomey?"

"Unh?"

She said, "I like you, Toomey. You're a very nice person." She kissed him again on the chest.

"I like it when you come to see me."

He grunted. Or something.

"Greg and Melanie like you, too. They told me so."

He didn't say anything.

She sighed, relaxed, sleepy. "You're good for me."

Again he grunted or something.

That was when she told him, with a tone of sincere regret in her voice, "I wish I loved you."

He said, "That's all right."

7

Toni Heller tossed a small gray suitcase into the back of the car, climbed behind the wheel, and twenty minutes later turned onto the Massachusetts Turnpike and headed east.

It was early Thursday morning, one week after Thanksgiving.

She was on her way.

She pulled into the first Howard Johnson's restaurant and service area she came to, but even before she came to a stop she was asking herself if this was only a stalling tactic. Do you really have to go to the bathroom?

She said, let's get on with it. You're out to get pregnant, and that's not going to happen in the restroom.

Not the women's restroom, anyway.

And it turned out that she was right, that she was only

stalling, because when she got to the restroom she found that she didn't have to go after all.

It had taken Toni a long time to decide where to go to look for the man she wanted.

Certainly not anywhere nearby, like Farmington or Amherst or Springfield. She didn't want to run into him a year from now in a supermarket or department store. Her shopping for diapers and pushing a baby carriage and him reminding her that they'd met once. Remember?

("About a year ago?"

"Yes, I remember."

"Beautiful baby. How old is it?"

"Three months."

"Three months, you say?")

She thought of New York City. And turned that down.

Boston? She rather liked that idea. Someone from one of the universities. Someone of high intelligence. And a high forehead, probably. And bad eyesight. But her eyes were good and maybe her boy would inherit his hair from her side of the family. And she remembered her father's bushy black hair.

(She reminded herself to hang on to her sense of humor. This isn't the easiest damn thing in the world you're doing, you know.)

Maybe she should continue past Boston, on out to the end of the Cape. To Provincetown. To some friendly bar where there would be a strong young fisherman with black curly hair, dark sparkling eyes, and a wide boyish grin. Full of spirit, good humor, looking for some fun.

But she shook that thought away.

This was not to be a romantic episode. She wanted no moments to remember. A year from now she'd want to no longer even be able to remember what her child's father had looked like. And she didn't want to know his name. Or where he was from or what he did for a living. Or anything about him that would make it possible for her to even consider going searching for him someday.

This was to be the first and last time she'd see him. That was a very definite part of her plan and she intended to keep it that way.

There was no reason why this should not be a pleasant experience. There was to be no crude coupling in an alley or in the back seat of an automobile. Nor with someone not attractive and decent. He would be, after all, the person her child would resemble and from whom he would inherit those characteristics that are passed down from a father to his child.

More than once she went down the list of things she'd like the man to be. Intelligent, tall, reasonably good looking, sensitive, and kind. From a family not burdened with inheritable health problems. And himself healthy, of course.

She had actually spent a lot of time simply deciding what to wear, and had ended up buying a new dress for the occasion. Her reasoning was that in a dress you can pick up the kind of man who really prefers to see his women wearing jeans and going barefoot. But the reverse maybe isn't always true. Or so she guessed.

The dress was a soft grayish green, casually stylish, comfortable, looked more expensive than it really was. It gave her the confidence that she needed. In the bedroom, when she tried it on, she looked in the full-length mirror and told herself that for an automobile mechanic she was still a pretty damn-good-looking woman.

And after she took the dress off she looked in the mirror some more and still felt good about it. Nothing there that she needed to be ashamed of.

She'd be able to walk into any place from here to Provincetown where there were men and once she let it be known that she was interested in letting one of them take her home, be able to choose from among the best of them.

She bought a small silver pin to wear with the dress, and silver earrings to match.

Okay, so sometimes a woman has to get dressed up to get the kind of man she wants. That's acceptable. You couldn't just go up to some man someplace and tell him that you'd like him to come out to your car for a minute. That you wanted to show him something. Wanted him to do something for you.

She didn't sleep much the night before. But in the morning she was able to laugh about that, too.

Well, she wanted to get to bed early tonight, anyway.

The sun was hot, the sky was clear blue, and the day was unusually warm for this time of year. That seemed a good sign and she suddenly found herself feeling very optimistic.

She was driving an old six-cylinder Dodge Dart that she had bought for a hundred and fifty dollars two weeks ago and had been working on in her spare time ever since. This was the first time she had had it on the highway. It was running beautifully, as she had known it would. But after she parked it in front of the Howard Johnson's, she raised the hood and spent a few moments looking at the motor. This, she told herself, was not part of any delaying tactics. This was because she wanted to take a look at all those parts that she had either repaired or put in new. Seeing the motor as it now was, and comparing it with what it had been like when she first got the car, gave her a good feeling of reassurance. She was seeing visible evidence that she was good at *something*, anyway.

Everyone needs that kind of feeling once in a while.

The man's voice behind her made her jump.

"Pardon me," he said. "Are you having trouble?"

Even before she turned around, he said, "I'm sorry. I startled you, didn't I?"

She said, "Right. You did." And was momentarily angry.

He said once more that he was sorry and she said once more that it was all right.

"But no. I'm not having trouble."

He was a big man, well over six feet, heavy, nothing particularly striking about him. Ordinary features, rather nice smile. Something about his expression gave you the feeling that he was a bit down about things.

He laughed, at himself, apparently, and said, "Foolish of me

60

to ask, anyway. I don't know anything about cars and couldn't have helped you even if I tried, probably."

She was tempted to agree. That it's foolish to offer help that you can't actually provide. But she restrained herself and simply said, "Well, thanks anyway."

Another man had now stopped, apparently to offer some help that he couldn't provide, so she put the hood down quickly before she became a major obstruction and point of interest on the sidewalk in front of the restaurant.

The man took the closing of the hood as a sign of dismissal and moved away.

She went into the bathroom but stayed only long enough to wash her hands and run a comb through her hair. On the way out, a voice inside her said, why don't you take time for a cup of coffee? But she shook her head.

She squeezed, with apologies, through the line of people buying coffee to take out, skirted around the line of people waiting to pay the cashier, and headed back to the car.

Outside, she looked up at the beautiful sky once more. And wondered what the weather on the Cape would be like. As good as it was here, she hoped.

Half a dozen cars beyond where her car was parked, a man had the hood up and was peering under it. As she got closer she saw that it was the man who had come by earlier to ask if she was having trouble. The big man. She saw him get back into his car, then come out a moment later and look under the hood again.

The voice inside her said that if she went over to ask him if she could help, it would only be another stalling tactic.

And she said that that wasn't true. You always help someone who needs help. And after he had shown concern when he thought she was having trouble, she couldn't possibly just get into her car and drive off.

When he saw her coming, he said, "Hi!" And laughed. "Now I'm the one who's having trouble."

She didn't bother to remind him that she hadn't *had* trouble. Just nodded to show that she remembered him. And moved over and stood beside him.

He asked, jokingly, "You know anything about motors?" And he tugged a bit on the battery cables, as probably he had done fourteen times already.

"A little."

He said, "That's more than I know." And pushed at the wires on the distributor cap.

"What happened when you tried to start it?"

He said, "All I got was a clicking noise."

He had expected more. That showed in his voice.

"Would you mind getting in and trying it once more?"

He did, and the result was what he had said. So she signaled him to turn off the key.

He got out and came over to her. Then he motioned toward where an attendant in the service area was putting gasoline into a car. "Maybe I'd better go see if they have a mechanic there who can tell me what the trouble is."

She didn't mind that he assumed that because she was a woman she didn't know anything about cars. Most women don't. As most men don't.

"Do you carry a screwdriver in your car?" He didn't think so. But maybe in the glove compartment. And he'd go look.

He did and he didn't.

So she went to her car and got one.

When she approached the car and was about to bend under the hood, he put out an arm and blocked her way.

"Your dress."

And she remembered. "Thanks." You don't work on a car when you're wearing a new dress with long loose sleeves.

"I don't want you to ruin your dress," he said. "Put my coat on."

That idea didn't appeal to her. She said, "I have an old sweater in the car. I'll put that on."

He offered to get it for her, so she let him.

She told him that it was on the front seat of the white Dodge Dart, but there were two other white cars near hers and he apparently didn't know a Dodge from any other kind and it was a little while before he was back with the sweater.

She asked him to get in the car and try it once more. And this time it started.

He waved excitedly, as if maybe to let her know that the car was running. And when she gestured for him to turn off the ignition he looked as if he didn't want to do so.

Turn it off, now that it was running?

She nodded. Yes.

He did, obediently, but reluctantly. Then got out and came around to where she was standing.

"What did you do?"

"I'll show you in a minute."

She heard herself speaking to him in very formal tones, like an instructor explaining something to a student.

"First," she said, "let me say that if you want to go over there to the service area, maybe they can fix it for you. But it will be more expensive here and you'll probably have to wait a long time. They probably won't have the part you need."

She looked down at the motor. "But if you prefer to go on to where you're going and have a garage there take care of it, I'll show you how to start it. Anytime you need to."

He looked undecided. "I don't know much about motors."

She said, "I know. Most people don't. But I'm not asking you to take the motor apart and put it back together again. What I'm going to show you, if you wish me to do so, is how to start the motor any time you need to until you get it to where you want to have it fixed."

He nodded. "I'd appreciate that."

She said, "All right." And bent over the motor.

"This," and she pointed with the screwdriver, "is called the solenoid. It's part of the starting system."

She tapped on it a couple of times. "You will probably have to replace it.

"Sometimes, though," she said, "you can fix it by reversing certain parts inside."

"I doubt if I could do that."

"I'm not suggesting you try."

What she was saying was coming out sounding hard and almost unfriendly. And she said to herself, for God's sake, relax. You're uptight.

"It's a job for a mechanic, of course. The point I was trying to make is that it isn't going to be a terribly expensive job. In case

63

that might have been worrying you."

He said that he was glad to hear that.

"Until you get it replaced or repaired, however, the way to start the car is to turn the ignition, with the car in neutral, of course, then come out here and put the screwdriver like this so it connects these two terminals." And she showed him what she meant. "These two points. Understand?"

She lay the screwdriver once more across the two points.

She went around to the driver's side, turned the key on, and came back to where he stood.

And she handed him the screwdriver.

He took it as if it were hot. Or had just been fished out of the toilet bowl.

After a small hesitation, he gingerly laid it across the terminals, and when the engine started he jumped back.

Then he grinned widely and said, "Hey! That's good."

"Do you think you can do it again the next time you need to?"

(You're still sounding like a school teacher, she said. Relax a little.)

He said, "I suppose I can do it, now that you've showed me how." And handed the screwdriver back to her.

She didn't take it.

"You'll need that, remember?"

He did. And laughed. And shook his head. "I'm sorry. I'm really dumb sometimes."

She noticed his hands as he closed the hood. They were big but not rough. Not the hands of a laboring man. And she wondered what he did for a living.

He was wearing a wrinkled light brown corduroy sports coat and a light blue shirt with no tie. Nice looking eyes and teeth. Nice smile. Strong face. He was looking at her with admiration.

"Where did you learn that trick? To start the car like that?"

She said, "I had three brothers."

And mentally got out the little list she'd made and looked at it.

He had noticed a small smudge on the sleeve of her sweater and that bothered him.

"I'm sorry about that."

"It will wash out," she said. And went back to studying her little list.

He was tall enough. Reasonably good looking. Looked healthy. And he had a relaxed and untroubled expression on his face of a kind that a person who is angry or mean doesn't end up with.

"I hope so," he said. "It looks like a nice sweater."

She said that she'd had it for years.

Intelligent? She would guess yes. Although you really couldn't tell.

"I'm lucky you happened to be here," he said. "And I thank you very much."

Had there been anything else on the list? Anything she'd forgotten?

He was holding out his hand. "Let me introduce myself."

She said, quickly, "Please don't."

His smile faded. He didn't understand. He slowly withdrew his hand and said, "Sorry."

He looked more confused than hurt.

"It's an old superstition," she said. "If you help a stranger, best not to know their name."

He hadn't known that. But he looked as if he could see that it made sense. And he apologized once more.

"But wait a minute before you go," she said. "Unless, of course, you're in a hurry."

He said he wasn't. Had all day. Hadn't even been headed anywhere in particular.

She turned away from him, lifted the hood up again, and looked at the motor once more. And had a small private talk with herself.

She probably wouldn't do much better than this. And could, quite possibly, if she tried to be too particular, end up doing much worse.

It was all a big gamble, anyway.

Besides, it would be a relief just to get started on it.

She put the hood back down, turned and held out her hand.

"Give me a name other than your real one."

The poor fellow looked at her. And for a moment said nothing.

Then, finally, in a low, tentative voice, he said, "John?"

They shook hands. Toni said, "Good to know you, John. I'm Maggie. Maggie Brown."

He selected Daniels. "John Daniels."

So that was settled. And they finished shaking hands.

"Thanks again for helping me. And for lending me the screwdriver."

"My pleasure."

He reached for his billfold. "Will you let me give you some money for it?"

She hesitated.

"I'd like to." And he held some bills in his hand. "Then you buy one for yourself to replace it."

Then he remembered, and added more bills. "And to get your sweater cleaned."

Toni pushed his hand away. "I wouldn't take your money, John."

"I'd like to give it to you."

"I won't take your money," she said. "But I've got an idea."

The poor fellow stood there, waiting, looking confused, still holding out the money, shoulders slumping a little.

He said, "What's your idea?"

"You did say that you were in no hurry?"

He nodded. He'd said that, all right. "I'm not headed anywhere in particular."

She said, "Then you could buy me lunch."

There wasn't much change of expression, but he nodded. Of course. Lunch.

Lunch was a good idea. Even though it was only ten o'clock in the morning.

"All right."

He looked over his shoulder toward the restaurant, then said, "Let me turn off my car, and I'll join you."

But she stopped him. "Let's not eat here," she said. "Let's find a place off the highway."

"Off the highway?"

She nodded.

"All right."

"Some place a little more interesting."

He said, "All right," again.

Toni said, "Just follow me in your car. I'll pick out a place."

That seemed all right with him. So she headed toward her car.

She looked back once and saw that he was still standing there, with the screwdriver in one hand and some money in the other, watching her. And she wondered if he would really follow her, or would he take the first chance to escape. Like simply continuing on his way when she turned off the turnpike.

She found that she hoped very much that he would follow her.

And he did. He followed her all the way.

Once when she went through a yellow light, he went through a red light so not to lose her.

She liked that.

8

Toomey kept his eyes on the white four-door sedan with the Massachusetts license plates on the back and a tall dark-haired girl inside. With a smudge on her sweater, three brothers, and no screwdriver.

The screwdriver was on the seat beside him. He touched it with his hand to reassure himself that all this was real and not some kind of crazy dream.

Even Madeline Toomey wouldn't have been able to predict this.

She might quite possibly have predicted that there would be a well-dressed and attractive dark-haired woman coming into his life, but she wouldn't, probably, have ventured to say that the woman would get his car started with a screwdriver, give it to him but not let him pay her for it, then ask him to take her to lunch somewhere off the turnpike.

All of which was rather strange.

But, unusual though it had been, Toomey felt satisfied that he had handled his part well enough. He had been casual and relaxed about the whole thing.

Lunch, you say, at some interesting restaurant off the turnpike at ten o'clock?

Well, a rather ordinary way for a person to start out on his vacation, but if that is what would amuse you to do, I'll be glad to join you.

And if at lunch it turned out that she was interested in getting him alone long enough to try to sell him some stock in a gold mine in Alaska, he'd handle that, too.

Just don't let it seem that you are surprised at what is happening. That's the secret.

Toomey remembered a former colleague named Clark Larmouth, with whom he'd been associated a few years ago.

Larmouth had been one of the few analysts Toomey had ever known who liked to talk about therapy techniques the way baseball players talk about how they grip the bat or place their feet at the plate or at precisely which moment they flip down the sunglasses when the long high one comes out of the sun.

Never, Larmouth said, let the patient think that anything he does or says surprises you. You've heard it all before, of course. Give the impression that you had in fact expected he or she would say just that very thing.

That gives the patient the feeling of confidence that comes from believing that you know exactly what his or her problems are, what he is going through, and just what it is that he must work out in his own head. Successfully, of course, as have the dozens and dozens who have come to you in the past with exactly the same kind of problem. A soft, amused smile of recognition on your part every once in a while helps convey this reassurance on your part. Or a barely perceptible nod of the head as he tells you of some absolutely unbelievable thing he is doing. Or feels or thinks.

Toomey saw the signal lights flashing on the right side of her car and slowed down. She turned off the turnpike at the next exit, and he followed. At the toll booth, as she paid her toll, he saw that she was asking the man in the booth a question and saw the man say something in response and make a gesture toward the east.

Toomey followed her as she headed in that direction, driving fast, passing cars, and he had to keep alert in order not to lose her.

After a while he found that he was wishing she would slow down a little. He watched the rearview mirror, keeping an eye out for police cars.

Once she went through a yellow light and to keep from losing her he had to go through on the red.

If it was lunch the young woman wanted, she was being rather particular where she had it. They passed restaurants of all kinds. Small intimate ones, large fancy ones. Quick service places like Burger Heaven and places that advertised beer and pizza.

Finally, however, she slowed down and pulled off the road and onto the grounds of what looked like a large hotel or resort. A big sign in front said Merritt Inn. It was a three-story brick building with a circular driveway and a small fountain in front in the center of a large oval flower bed with a low wall around it. A few people were sitting on the low wall, watching the fountain or just talking. A number of other people were carrying bags into or out of the building. Well-dressed people, mostly. Many of them young. Vacationers, newlyweds, professional or business men attending a convention or conference or some such thing.

But if this is where she wanted her lunch, that was all right with him. She had rescued him and he was grateful. He would do all that he could to see that she had a good lunch.

She had found space in the parking lot and had already got out of her car when he pulled alongside her.

It took a little courage to turn off the motor, which she noticed. And she smiled.

"It's all right."

He said, "I hope I can start it up again."

"Don't worry," she said. "You will."

She said, "You started it once, so you can do it again."

They made their way through the lobby, which was not especially crowded, and on to the dining room, which was not crowded at all. Less than half a dozen tables in the large room were occupied, people finishing a late breakfast, probably, and at a far end of the room were several waitresses sitting with coffee and cigarettes.

They took a table on the side, and looked around.

"Do you like it?"

Toomey said that he did. "Very pleasant place. You picked a good spot."

He looked around at the soft lighting, attractive murals, and general air of elegance.

"You come here often?"

One of the waitresses at the end of the room crushed out her cigarette, got up, and started in their direction.

She said that this was the first time she'd been here.

"I've never even been on this road before."

Before the waitress arrived, Toomey asked if she thought it was too early in the day to have a drink before eating, and she said that she thought not. She'd had the same idea, in fact.

She ordered a bottle of beer, so that was what he ordered, too. The waitress, a serious, unsmiling woman about Toomey's age, maybe a little older, didn't seem too happy about that. People ordering beer this time of morning weren't exactly measuring up to the style and class the Merritt Inn expects of its guests. But she took their order.

They agreed on one of the more expensive brands of beer, Toomey reminding her that he was picking up the check and that he wanted her to have the best.

After the waitress had gone, they both leaned back and relaxed. And Toomey took time for a closer look at the young woman who had rescued him and his car.

She was not especially beautiful, but something about the face was very attractive. Although it was a bit too long and the nose a little too thin, and the strong white teeth attracted more attention than most beauty consultants would have recommended, he liked it. The smile was nice. The kind that you almost automatically smile back at.

She was wearing a soft grayish green dress that was close to the color of her eyes. And a thin silver necklace that matched a small silver pin. The outfit looked new, as if it had been bought for a special occasion. And he wondered where she was heading. A friend's wedding, probably. Or to spend the weekend with someone she was fond of. Like a favorite uncle. Who maybe had a lot of money.

He was pretty sure it was one or the other.

So he asked, "Where were you going before you interrupted your trip to help out a stranded motorist?"

But before she could answer, he said, "Let me guess."

"All right."

He said, "My first guess would be to a wedding."

He could tell that that was not far wrong. She looked thoughtful, tilted her head a little to one side, and said, "That's close. Something like that.

"Not really a wedding, though."

Toomey was satisfied. Close is pretty good.

"My second guess," Toomey said, "would have been that you were going to see someone you like very much and who is important to you. Like perhaps a favorite uncle who happens to have a lot of money."

She said, "How about the wedding anniversary of a favorite uncle who has a lot of money?"

Toomey nodded. He said, "I knew it was something like that."

And they smiled at each other.

He looked down at her hands. There were no rings.

She said, "I hope I haven't taken you too far out of your way."

He said that she hadn't. "I wasn't heading anywhere in particular. Just going on a small vacation."

He told her that he had thought of going out to the Cape somewhere. "Stroll along the beach," he said, "and let the wind blow through the holes in my head."

He had not meant the remark to be taken seriously, but she seemed bothered by it.

"Aren't you feeling well?"

"Physically," he said, "I'm in perfect health."

She seemed glad to hear that. "And other than physically?"

"Dumb, is all."

She leaned back again and smiled. "You don't look dumb."

The waitress was back and set two bottles of beer on the table.

"Well, I am. At least I seem to do a lot of dumb things."

The waitress placed a menu in front of each of them. Breakfast menus. And when they said that it was lunch they wanted, her face hardened again. And her expression showed that they were really testing her patience. And she explained that they didn't start serving lunch until eleven-thirty.

Toomey said that they'd wait.

He looked across the table at her. "Is that all right with you?"

She said that it was.

The waitress silently took back the menus, frowned once more, and left.

He filled her glass for her and then his own. He said, "This is a nice way to spend a morning. I feel like I'm on vacation."

She said that she felt that way, too, and they raised their glasses in a toast to vacation feelings.

"What I like best about having lunch this time of morning," Toomey said, "is that you always have to have a couple drinks while you wait."

She seemed amused at that. But admitted that she had never before gone to lunch quite this early.

"It's the best time," Toomey said. "Believe me."

And they both had a sip of their beer.

Then she went back to pick up on something he had said earlier.

"What is it you do that's so dumb?"

He said that he wouldn't know where to begin. Then he got out a cigar and asked her if it was all right. And she nodded. Of course. And took a cigarette from a pack in her purse.

She said, "You look intelligent."

Toomey thought about that for a moment.

"Well educated, anyway. Good universities."

"Don't tell me which ones."

He said, "Of course not. Knowing where I went to school would bring you seven years of bad luck."

She said, "Eight. It would be eight because you went to more than one."

She was looking at him thoughtfully across the top of her glass.

"You aren't working now?"

He said that he wasn't, but that he planned to go back to work soon. It was mostly a matter of deciding where he wanted to go to get started again.

She studied him another moment or two, then said, "You can tell me what kind of work you did, but not who you worked for. And don't be too specific."

"All right." And thought a moment.

"The place I worked longest was in Connecticut. Is that all right to say?"

"You've already said it. Just don't name the city."

"It wasn't a city," he said. "A small town that I'm sure you never heard of."

After another moment, he said, "I dealt with people."

"You're a professional card player."

That was good, and he laughed. And shook his head. "No. It wasn't that exciting an occupation."

He said, "These were sick people."

"Maybe you shouldn't tell me any more."

He said, "No, that's all right. I won't tell you what it is. But I'm interested in seeing if I can describe it without telling what it is."

After another drink of beer and a little thought, he said, "One thing is that you have to know a lot of definitions. Also, you have to have a lot of patience."

That small pun was unintended, and he smiled. Then continued. "You have to have enough self-discipline to keep your mouth shut most of the time. And not give too much advice. At least, that's the way most people in my line of work think. I tend to take a somewhat different approach."

He said, "And you have to be encouraging and supportive and not fall asleep when you get bored at hearing excuses that

75

you've heard a thousand times before."

She said, rather sharply, he thought, "That's enough. Don't tell me any more."

He nodded. "All right." And they both had a sip of their beer.

He asked her what she did when she wasn't rescuing motorists, and noticed that she looked down at her hands. They were hands that looked as if they were used. Strong. A bit rough.

"Would you believe that I was an Avon lady?"

He shook his head.

"I would ordinarily," he said, "because you have nice hands. But I decided on the way here that you are a race driver."

She shook her head.

"Either that or your father's a judge or the head of the Massachusetts State Police."

She laughed, shook her head, switched the questions back to him.

"Did your doctor suggest you get away for a rest?"

He said that he hadn't been to a doctor for years. "Not since I got out of college. It's an understanding we have. They don't meddle in my affairs and I don't meddle in theirs."

She seemed to approve of that.

"You must come from a healthy family."

He told her that everyone in his family had been strong and healthy for generations.

She thought that was good.

"They don't, however, tend to live to a ripe old age."

That wasn't so good. She asked, "Why?"

"I don't know. It just happens."

He said, "Like my father, who drowned in a canoe race on the Wabash River at age sixty-seven."

She nodded approvingly. Apparently she thought that that was a nice way to go.

"But my mother," he said, "got to be relatively old. Even though she was never quite the same after she fell off the ladder and broke her hip."

"At age seventy-four. Fixing the roof."

He said, "No. Just hanging wallpaper. And she wasn't

seventy-four. Closer to seventy, I'd say."

So they each had some more beer.

"Did many members of your family die of inherited diseases? Like diabetes, heart trouble, cancer, or Parkinson's disease?"

Toomey said, "In the small town I came from people didn't have diseases that were hard to spell. People there mostly had the flu. Or were simply ailing."

He said, "Most people died simply from just ailing too long."

"Don't tell me the name of the town."

All this was amusing and Toomey felt better than he'd felt for a long time. He told her that.

"This is one of the most pleasant lunches I've ever had," he said. "And I haven't even had it yet."

She laughed at that. She said, "I'm glad. I'm enjoying it, too."

She added, "Where I usually eat it's ordinarily not quite as pleasant as this."

He said, "Don't tell me where it is."

A moment later he finished his beer and set the glass down and looked at her.

"We have another half hour or so before they serve lunch. Do you want another beer?"

She said she thought not.

"Is it all right if I have one?"

She didn't answer him. Not directly, anyway. What she did was reach out her hand and put it on top of his. And held it there. And looked into his eyes.

She said, "I like you, John. I really do. You're a very nice person. I like your sense of humor. You're fun to be with."

All he could think of to say was, "Thank you."

And he wondered how it could be that he was so dumb that it had taken him all this time to figure out what was happening.

This attractive young woman wasn't going to try to sell him real estate in Florida or a gold mine in Alaska.

She was simply trying to pick him up.

Toomey remembered a patient he'd had a few years ago

77

who did this kind of thing. Her name was Thelma. Thelma something or other. Right at this moment he couldn't remember her last name. But she had been one of his favorite patients of all time.

A young woman about the same age as this one sitting across from him. From a very religious family. Not particularly attractive, but neither was she especially unattractive. She was slender, wore glasses, was shy, had a dull job, and only women friends. No boyfriends. And couldn't deal with the intimacy of sex. Before coming to Toomey she had not gone to any other person for help for her problem. Instead, with what one had to admit showed more courage than good sense, she had started working on the problem by herself as best she could.

She had tried to make herself less afraid of sex by making herself do it. Always with men she'd never seen before and would never see again. She wouldn't pick up men locally, but went out of town to bars or restaurants or nightclubs. She'd tell them nothing about herself nor let them tell her anything about themselves. Everything was to be as unintimate as possible. No personal relationship. Love with the lights out and her being passive and noninvolved, all in the hope—or so she thought—that after a while she would accept the fact that having sex with a man was something that one could get used to.

The problem was that the men she let take her home or to a motel weren't always as nice as they had seemed at first to be.

And, even worse, what she was honest enough to recognize, was that after a while she was beginning to not mind that some of them rather enjoyed knocking her around a bit.

Toomey had been able to help her. That was one of his nice memories. It had taken nearly a year, but by the time she had finished her treatment she was going with a good man to whom she had been making good love for two months and they were engaged to be married. And by now she had no doubt graduated to mirrors and water beds.

He asked, "How about you? Have you been to a doctor lately? If so," he added, "don't tell me his name."

She said, "I've had no reason to."

She was still holding his hand.

"Parkinson's disease, cardiac arrest, or Huntington's Chorea?"

She said, "I've never been arrested for anything in my life. And never out of the country."

He nodded approvingly.

"How's your sex life?"

"It's been a while."

He was about to spare her some embarrassment by being the first to suggest that they go to bed together. But she beat him to it.

"I don't want another beer," she said. "And I'm not really hungry."

"No?"

"What I really want," she said, "is to go to bed with you."

She rubbed his hand softly. "If you will."

He said, "I'd like that."

He put a hand across hers and squeezed it a little. "I was about to ask you the same thing."

And they smiled at each other.

He signaled to the waitress. And when she got to the table he asked for the check.

He said that they'd changed their minds about lunch. And since they were still holding hands, she seemed to understand.

This being more in accord with the expected behavior of guests at the Merritt Inn, she didn't frown at them. She almost smiled.

Toomey registered them as Mr. and Mrs. John Daniels.

9

Before calling Glenna and Angela into his office, Toomey cleared a space in the middle of his desk, got the shot glass from the drawer and placed it upside down in the center of the large green blotter. He lowered the window shade to darken the office and took the telephone receiver off the cradle so not to be disturbed. Then he leaned back, put his feet up on the desk, relaxed, took some deep breaths, focused on the shot glass, half closed his eyes, and waited casually for the feelings and images to come through.

He took Glenna first.

There came vague feelings of turbulence. Wild thrashing about. Childish defiance and adult demands and tears and screams and doors slamming and bruises slow to heal. Scars, bars, chips flying and gradually emerging like a reflection in a pool of water calmed after the stones have stopped, a face made up of angry pieces, angular, shaped by shaking hands from clay that hardened too quickly.

He saw her struggling to break free of motorcyclists in black leather jackets. He saw her shouting angry words. In and out of the home. Defiance, stubbornness, recklessness. Flirting with someone at a carnival. Drugs and drink and her in tears and in trouble somewhere in the Middle West. Peoria seemed to come through. But he couldn't be sure.

It might have been East St. Louis.

He waited a little longer but nothing more came. Nothing to indicate what she would be like when she grew up. Or if she ever did.

He opened his eyes, got up for a moment, walked over and patted Roman on the head. Walked once around the room, then went back to the desk and took the same position as before.

Angela.

There came soft shapes. Pinkness and smiles and laughter. Playground swings and things that make a small girl's eyes grow big. A father's arms outstretched and cross words overheard and sobs it didn't hurt to hear. Parties that threatened to end too soon. And balloons.

The face that came through was pink and twenty-eight and saying no. Never. Tied at the end of a rope, at the highway's edge, with her thumb in the air.

He saw her, too, struggling to break free. Flinging herself about. He saw a middle-aged salesman, short, fat, balding, angry with her, finally. In a motel room somewhere in the East. New Jersey, it seemed like. Abandoned at a motel without money for food or bus fare. Then he saw her going back to her parents. Boston. A country club. And a young man, with things working out well in the end.

He got up, raised the window shade, put the phone back on the cradle, and looked out on the lake for a moment.

Then he put the shot glass back into the drawer and went out to ask Mrs. Murphey to have Glenna and Angela come in to see him sometime today when it was convenient.

Back in his office he mentioned to Roman that he would like to take a little walk by the lake after he'd talked to the girls and Roman thumped his tail to remind Toomey that he'd want to come along.

Glenna, when she came in, apparently assumed that she was about to be fired.

Even before she sat down, she said, "I was planning to quit this dumb job anyway. So if you're going to fire me, go ahead. I don't care."

Toomey said, "That's not what I had in mind, Glenna. But sit down a minute."

Glenna was about average height, slender, with sharp features that were made to appear more so by the wire-rimmed glasses she wore. Although none of the separate parts of her face was top rate, she was not unattractive. But she could be, as was obvious, much more pleasant to look at. An occasional warm smile would do wonders. Instead of the suggestion of a snarl that hovered about her mouth. Her hair, long and the color of dark honey, fell down over her face. She would pull it to one side and a moment later it would fall down again. She gave the impression of one who periodically looked briefly out upon the world, found it distasteful, and withdrew.

"I'm sorry you're not happy with the job," Toomey said. "And I can understand why."

He said, "It's not the most exciting job in the world. Everyone gets tired of it after a while."

"Mrs. Murphey is a jerk."

Toomey told her that he didn't agree with that.

"And if you'd take time to get to know her, you'd find that she's really a very fine person."

She combined the look on her face with a noise in her throat to convey how little respect she had for his opinion.

"I suppose she's been complaining that I don't make enough baskets."

Toomey admitted that that was partly true. "But it's been so hot lately that we aren't blaming anyone for not working as hard as usual."

"It's awful hot out there. No air conditioning or anything."

83

She looked so unattractive when she twisted her mouth around like that. Toomey winced a little.

"What I wanted to talk to you about," he said, "was not Mrs. Murphey, but your friends on their motorcycles who pick you up after work. Mrs. Boughton, across the street, has been complaining about the noise."

"Oh, my God!" She took a package of cigarettes from her shirt pocket.

"So that's what's bugging you."

She almost smiled. As if pleased to find she had done something that annoyed him. Good!

"I have the right to meet anybody I want," she said, "anywhere I want to."

She didn't seem to have a light, so Toomey handed her a package of matches.

"I'm not saying your friends can't meet you after work," he said.

She started to hand the matches back, but he said, "Keep them. I have more."

Then he said, "Mrs. Boughton is an old woman and shouldn't have to have her nerves shattered every afternoon at five o'clock by three or four noisy motorcycles in front of her house."

"Mrs. Boughton is an old bitch."

Toomey kept his patience. He said, "All you have to do is ask them to park at the corner by the gas station. And turn off their motors. That's simple enough."

In a more serious tone, he added, "If Mrs. Boughton makes too many complaints to the selectmen about this shop, they may want to take another look at whether or not we should even be here."

She didn't say anything, so he repeated his request. "Will you ask the kids to pick you up at the corner?"

She started laughing.

He said, "It isn't funny, Glenna. Mrs. Boughton has her rights. And the selectmen already have a number of people complaining about this place. And if they close us down a number of nice people will be out of work."

She said, "That wasn't what I was laughing about. I was laughing at what Scooter and Cruiser would say if they heard you refer to them as kids."

Toomey took a deep breath and let several seconds pass before continuing. He said, "All right. I'll not call them kids. And I'm not saying that they aren't good fellows. But just tell them to pick you up on the corner from now on."

She said, "I saw what they did to one man who gave them some lip."

That was almost too much, but Toomey kept the same relaxed expression on his face.

"Anyway, in order to save trouble for all of us who work here, please ask them not to pick you up in front anymore."

As much as half a minute, maybe, passed before either of them spoke.

Then she asked, "Can I go now?"

He said, "Don't go yet. Let's talk some more about the job. There must be some way I can get you to feel better about it."

He reached into the drawer and pulled out a cigar.

She said, "I don't want to hear it."

And repeated the question, "Can I go now?"

He opened the drawer once more and pitched the cigar back in.

He said, "Sure. Go back to work. But if you give Mrs. Murphey any more lip I'll have to fire you."

As she got up and headed for the door, she looked back at him and said, "My advice to you is, don't give the Hornets a hard time."

After she had gone, Toomey wasted a few moments questioning whether he might have handled things better. But he didn't see how else he could have talked to her, and after a while put the incident out of his mind.

At noon, when he took Roman for a walk down to Harvey's, he bought two dozen pencils and one of the little-league baseball bats that Harvey stocked. Light, but had a nice balance to it. He liked the feel of it so much that he went back later and bought a second one to keep at the house.

Harvey said, "You taking up baseball?"

Toomey said no. "Just buying it for some kids."

While he was there he remembered he needed some crayons, too.

After lunch, Angela Coates came into the office.

Angela was large, blond, soft flesh, and pinkness. She was twenty-eight but looked twenty-one. She had been adopted as an infant by a Boston couple. Her father was a circuit court judge and her mother a guidance counselor at a high school on the north side. Angela had attended art schools off and on and had put in a year at an expensive private mental hospital near Worcester.

Angela was not as inexperienced in the ways of the world as her cherubic expression might lead a person to believe. She had lived for two years with a man old enough to be her father. She had hitchhiked around the country with young men her own age. And before coming to Baskets and Baskets had been traveling with a group of people selling magazine subscriptions door to door.

Mrs. Murphey had told him, when he hired her four weeks ago, that she wouldn't work out. But Toomey said that Angela had told him she needed money to get home. When a person has been away for a year, he said, you can't expect that person to go home without good clothes and money in her pocket. And besides, the Reverend Osterman had asked him to give her a job.

The weeks had passed, however, and she hadn't bought any clothes or made plans for going home. And all she talked about was how everyone who worked here was crazy and how she was going to kill herself.

When she came into the office Toomey asked her how things were going and she said, "Terrible."

"What's the matter?"

"I can't stand all these sick people. And I know that if I don't get out of here soon I'm going to kill myself."

He reached into the drawer for a cigar and started unwrapping it.

"I can't stand this place any longer."

He said, "Of course not. Because you don't belong here. You should this afternoon be out on some sunny hillside painting a landscape in brilliant greens and golden browns and clear sky blues. Not in the stuffy shop weaving baskets."

"I can't paint," she said. "You know that."

"That's not true."

A few weeks ago, shortly after she had started work, she had come in one morning with some bright-colored drawings and hung them along the walls with Scotch tape. Although hastily done and too quickly finished, they got a favorable response from everyone in the shop. But that afternoon, after everyone had told her how much they liked them, she had torn them from the wall and thrown them into the wastebasket.

"I can't paint. I can't do anything."

Toomey said, "There's lots of things you can do." And he lit the cigar.

"There's one thing you can do for me," he said.

She didn't say anything.

"I want you to take a week off and go see your father and mother. They haven't seen you for over a year, I heard you say. So I know how worried about you they must be."

"They aren't worried about me."

He said, "Of course they are." And tossed the match toward the wastebasket.

"What I'm going to do is advance you a week's salary. You go home and show your parents that you're well and happy, looking fine. Then come back here.

"Or," he added, "if you decide to stay, keep the week's salary as a gift from me. Count it as severance pay, or something."

"They don't want me to come home. I told you that once."

"Of course they do."

"They just want me to go back to the hospital."

He said, "Eventually, they might. Sooner or later they may suggest you go back for a while. Or to a private therapist. But that isn't what they'll want you to do right away.

"What they'll want you to do right away is go out with them to dinner and the theatre and places like that. To the ocean. The beach."

"They don't have time to do those things. They both work."

"Well, they don't work all the time."

She sort of grunted softly to show that he didn't know them as well as she did.

"Do you have any brothers or sisters? Or friends in Boston?"

She said, "I've been thinking about killing myself."

His cigar had not gone out, but he touched a match to the tip of it anyway. And waved the match in the air violently a half dozen times.

"Look, Angela," he said. "I know what you're going through. But it so happens that I know how things are going to turn out for you."

He said, "You're going to go home pretty soon. Back to your parents. And you're going to lie around for a while, just being fed and cared for."

He interrupted himself and leaned forward to ask a question. "Your parents belong to a country club, don't they?"

She nodded.

He leaned back in his chair. "I thought so."

He said, "Anyway, at the country club you're going to meet a young man who's gone through the same kind of problems you've gone through. You'll become fond of each other, impatient with each other from time to time. But always helpful to each other. And one of these days you'll get married, have two kids, and they'll both be talented and successful and you'll be proud of them."

There was a period of silence before she spoke.

"I'm going to commit suicide."

That sounded like a final decision, but he refused to accept it.

"I don't think you're going to."

"I'm going to."

He looked out the window. "The day is beautiful, things are growing, kids are playing, lovers are holding hands, and tired businessmen from New York and Boston are racing their stupid motorboats back and forth on the lake."

He turned back to her. "Go back into therapy, Angela. But instead of concentrating so much on yourself and your own problems, use the experience as a way of getting a bigger view of things."

He said, "See it all. And how it is all right. A damn good rose garden, actually. With thorns, bugs, and worms in the ground, I admit. But beautiful. And fragrant.

"Enjoy it."

She refused to look at him.

"I'm going to commit suicide."

Toomey shrugged his shoulders to show that if that was what she wanted to do, there wasn't anything he could do about it.

"All right. If you want to kill yourself, then do it. It's been done before. No big deal. But it would be dumb. And I hope you don't."

He said, "The better solution would be to head back to Boston and find that young man who's looking for you and wants to marry you and have two children."

A little later Mrs. Murphey came in to say that Angela had left the shop, that she had been very upset and was telling everyone that she was going to kill herself and that it was "all Mr. Bougereau's fault."

"That's too bad," Toomey said.

"But," he added, "at least that clears you. She's no longer saying that it will be all your fault."

That thought did seem to make Mrs. Murphey feel a little better. The burden was now shifted from her to Toomey.

"Well, I hope she doesn't."

Toomey said, "Me, too."

It wasn't even the middle of the afternoon, but he opened the desk drawer and took out a bottle. He poured himself the smallest possible amount of bourbon into a paper cup. Hardly enough to wet the bottom. So little that if he hadn't downed it immediately it would probably have evaporated.

"It's a rough life, Roman," Toomey said. And Roman thumped his tail to show that he agreed with that.

"Having to lie on the hard floor all day," Toomey said, "is no bed of roses."

He called his sister, Ethel, that evening.

89

"How are things in Angora?"

"How were they when you left?" she said. "Nothing's changed here since then."

"How's the fishing been this summer?"

She said, "Now, Toomey, how in hell would I know how the fishing's been? I still got four teen-age girls at home to take care of, you know."

He said, "You sound tired."

She said she wasn't. No more than usual, anyway. "You sound like you've been drinking."

He said, "Not at all. Not much, anyway."

He said, "I've been watching this show on TV where the police chase some criminal in a Ford Fairlane onto the Indianapolis Speedway and they are chasing him around the track and they catch him when he has to pull over for a pit stop.

"It reminded me of you," he said, "because I know how you and Ed always go to the five-hundred-mile races every year."

She said, "Toomey." And after a moment, "When are you going to quit that damn foolishness and go back to work?"

"I'm thinking of it."

She said, "Good."

"I think I'm going back to Angora and work."

She said, "I got a better idea. Set up an office in Indianapolis and come here weekends and take the girls fishing. They'd really like that."

He said that he thought that was a good idea. "In the meantime, ask people where the good fishing places are these days. I had in mind some of those creeks back off the road a ways. Places where the catfish are biting."

She promised she'd do that. "And do me a favor, will you?"

He said, "I've already done it. I've cut way back. I don't drink hardly at all anymore."

"That's good. And take care of yourself."

He said he would. And that he'd call her again next week.

She said, "Good."

They both said good-bye.

Angela didn't come to work the next day. And the day after

that, while Toomey was in Boston delivering a load of baskets, Reverend Osterman, from the First Church in Farmington, came to the shop looking for her. He said that he had been counseling her and that she'd called the day previous and had said that she was going to commit suicide.

Glenna offered the information that Angela had finally decided to kill herself because Mr. Bougereau had told her that it was all right to do so.

10

As they left the dining room and walked into the lobby, Toni was suddenly aware that for the first time since Thanksgiving the tension was gone.

It had all been so easy. And might even turn out to be rather nice, the rest of it.

Even his awkwardness and seeming innocence made things better.

He had started over to the desk to register and she had had to call him back.

"John?"

He stopped and turned, "Yes?"

She walked up to him and said in a low voice, "Don't you think we should get our luggage from the car?"

He said, "Of course. You'll need your bag."

"It's not that I'll need my bag," she said. "It's just that it will look better if we have luggage."

He'd forgotten that. "Of course." And he shook his head at his dumbness.

He had her wait in the lobby, took her keys, and returned a little later with her bag and his.

Next, he gave the clerk the name John Daniels, without a moment's hesitation, as if he had been using the name all his life. Then proceeded to write out a personal check for the amount. Then stood there, looking foolish, no doubt feeling the same, holding out the check with his real name on it, whatever it was. Then slowly withdrawing it.

"I think I'll just pay you in cash."

The clerk, a thin young man in a white shirt, black bow tie, and the maroon jacket that was apparently the prescribed uniform at Merritt Inn, said, "All right, sir."

John got some bills from his wallet, gave them to the clerk, and got back his change.

"Thank you, Mr. Daniels," he said. And turned over the key. And looked at both of them.

"Have a good time."

John said, "Thank you." And he took her bag and his and they headed for the elevator.

She liked the room. It was big and bright and had two large windows. One window overlooked the patio and swimming pool, which was now empty, of course, and the other provided a view of open fields and distant hills.

The windows shades were up, but she raised them even higher, letting the sun flood the room and brighten the hue of the yellow flowers on the white wallpaper. There was a lamp by the bed. She turned that on.

"Do you like it?"

He said, "Yes. Do you?"

"Very much."

She looked at the big man and smiled. This was nice. She had made a good choice.

An hour or two from now she would be on her way back to Coultraine, with the start of something nice inside her. Mission accomplished. And he would be on his way to wherever he had been headed for before they met.

"It's all very nice," she said. "I'm glad we met."

He said, "Me, too."

Then he asked if it was all right if he called room service and had them send up a bottle of wine. Or two.

She said that he could, if he liked. So he made the call. He ordered one bottle, then changed it to two.

He had first asked her what kind of wine she liked and she said that she didn't care.

"A dry white wine?"

"Perfect."

Anything. She hadn't come here to drink wine. She had wine at home. What she had come here for was that man there just now hanging up the phone.

The innocent! And she laughed.

"What are you laughing at?"

She said, "I'm sorry. I was just remembering how embarrassed you looked when you told the clerk that your name was John Daniels and then started to hand him a check with your real name on it."

They both laughed for a moment. And he said, "I told you that I was dumb."

"It didn't show that at all," she said. "It only shows that you don't very often register at hotels under a different name."

He said that it was the first time. And looked at her.

So she told him it was her first time, too.

She didn't bother to open her suitcase. He didn't open his. And they didn't say much. They admired the views. Agreed that during the summer months it probably was very enjoyable down there by the pool, having lunch or drinks at the table, in and out of the water, enjoying the sun. Except that the pool was located on the side of the hotel where the shadows fell first. It would have been better, they agreed, if it had been on the other side of the building, facing the setting sun.

They also agreed that there was something good about being here during the off season, with not too many people around and everything comparatively quiet.

There was a brochure on the table describing the inn and they looked at it together. There was an indoor swimming pool, a handball court, and a steam room for women and one for men. There was a recreation room with a Ping-Pong table, darts, chess boards, pinball machines, and anything else the vacationer, businessman, or newlywed might want.

Ideal for large parties, conventions, conferences.

The cuisine, it said, was excellent. And there was a picture of the chef. French. A small moustache and a tall white hat.

She thought he seemed a bit relieved when the wine came. It gave him something to do. Opening the bottle and filling the glasses.

There seemed to be a rapport between him and the bottles and the glasses that caused her to ask, for no particular reason, "Do you drink a lot?"

He said, "Not too much. But more than I should, probably."

She wasn't bothered by that, drinking not being hereditary. As far as she knew.

They touched their glasses together. She couldn't think of an appropriate toast, and neither could he, apparently, so there was no toast.

He drained his glass quickly. She took a little longer. And a nice warm feeling came across her.

They were standing by the window that looked out upon the hills and fields.

"I like the hills," he said. "The part of the country I came from was very flat."

She knew that with a little encouragement he would tell her all about it. So she kept quiet.

They had now been there maybe twenty minutes. He hadn't even touched her. So she touched him. She put a hand on his arm and stroked it gently.

"The wine was a good idea."

He thought so, too. And poured himself some more. He held the bottle up, but she said, "Not yet. In a moment."

Then she said, "Why don't you bring your wine to bed?" And, as he took a sip from the glass, added, "Bring the bottle, too. If you'd like."

Which was what he would have done anyway, probably. "Okay."

He asked if she'd like to use the bathroom first, and she said no. She'd just get into bed.

He went to the bathroom, probably to give her time to get undressed and into bed. So she did that. And when he came back she had the covers drawn up and the sheet demurely tucked beneath her chin.

He went over to one of the windows and pulled the shade down.

And she said, "Oh!" in a tone that meant she wished he wouldn't.

He paused, turned and looked at her. "I thought you would want the shades down."

She said, "Pull them down, if you like. But it's rather nice having the bright sun coming in."

So he raised the shade back up.

So she, as if to compromise, turned off the lamp by the bed.

She watched while he got undressed. That nice, non-threatening, nonaggressive, almost shy person that pure good luck had provided her.

In a few moments she was going to take that big man and hold him and warm him and relax him and squeeze him until he filled her with what she had come here to get.

"Come to bed."

He said, "Coming."

He had undressed with his back to her. And now he was getting into bed as if trying to reveal no more of his nakedness than necessary.

She almost laughed.

He poured more wine for them both, and they leaned on one elbow and clinked their glasses together.

He asked if she was using some kind of birth control and she said that she was, of course. Which was an innocent untruth.

"I wouldn't want you to get pregnant if you didn't want to."

She said, "Me either." Which was true.

He had a sip of wine and said, "I haven't been with any women of the kind I need to worry about."

She said, "I don't have any contagious diseases either." And took a quick sip of wine to keep from laughing.

From the terrace below there came the sound of people laughing. Young couples, it sounded like. Playing some game and enjoying it.

That was nice. She liked games. People having fun. And she reached out a hand and stroked her good friend on the shoulder. Then moved the hand down and let it rest on his stomach.

He said, "I like you."

That, too, she assumed, was intended to make her feel better.

"I like you, too."

That seemed to please him.

He had more wine, then asked, "This is not the first time for you, of course?"

She did choke on her wine that time, and he apologized.

"I guess that was a dumb question."

She said that it wasn't, really.

"Of course you've made love before."

She said, "Once!" And then she did laugh and spilled wine on the pillow.

Someone, either the management or a former occupant, had left a box of Kleenex on the table by her and she took one and blotted at the wine a moment.

She said, "Sorry." As if it were his pillow or something.

"That's all right."

She said, "What I was laughing at was an old joke I just remembered."

He seemed to want to hear it, so she told it to him.

"It's the joke about the young woman who filled out an application for a job for some company. It asked for things like her name, age, height, sex, and so forth. You've heard it, I'm sure."

He said that he hadn't.

She told him how she had happened to hear some comedian use it on a late night TV show back when she was in high school. "The woman gave her name, Jennie Jones, age twenty-two, height five-six, weight one-twenty. And under sex put 'Once in Munsen, Massachusetts.'"

He thought that was very funny and laughed hard for a few moments.

"Everyone in Munsen," she said, "laughed about it for days."

She set her glass of wine on the table on her side of the bed and settled down to business. She had not come here to tell jokes.

She ran a hand along his body from his chest down to his thighs. You couldn't tell just by feeling whether or not he was fertile, but he certainly wasn't impotent. And she gave him a little squeeze there.

He put a hand on her breast, tentatively, as if not sure that it was all right to do so. She put her hand on top of his and pressed, just to show that it not only was all right, but that it was really very pleasant. And she could feel her nipple growing hard against the palm of his hand.

He pulled back a little. And looked at her.

He said, "Maggie, I think maybe I had you figured out wrong." And he reached back to take up his glass of wine again.

She tried not to be impatient with him. According to her calculations, if he would just make love to her sometime within the next forty-eight hours it would be all right.

She said, "That's possible." And took a sip of her wine, too.

She was about to ask him, just for curiosity's sake, how it was that he had figured her out, anyway, but now he had something else that he must have felt he needed to say to make her feel better.

"I'm not married."

She said, "That's good. That makes me feel better."

"I used to be, though. Not that it's important."

"Really?"

He said, "Twice."

She continued to be patient. Even though she was now down to only forty-seven hours and fifty-nine minutes. She sipped her wine.

"Do you have children?"

"No."

That was a little sobering. She sat up in bed. She set the glass on the table and looked at him.

"You were married twice but had no children?"

"No."

"Did you try?"

This time he was the one who laughed and spilled a little of his wine on the sheet.

"Sorry."

She said, "That's all right." And took another Kleenex from the box and blotted at the wine spot.

"That was clumsy of me."

She said that it wasn't. And not to worry about it.

"But," she said, "I'm curious about whether you wanted children and couldn't have them."

He said, "I wanted them, all right. I've always wanted children."

"Then why didn't you have them? Was it because you couldn't? Or your wives couldn't?"

He said, "My first wife felt that she was needed in the career she was in and didn't have time for children."

All right.

"How about the second?"

"She already had four. She didn't want more."

She gave a deep sigh. Took the glass from the table, drained it, and set it aside. And turned to him.

"Put your wine away, John."

That was a direct order.

He did as she demanded. First finishing off what was left in the glass, of course.

Then he, too, seemed to settle down to business.

He kissed her the way she liked to be kissed. And the pounding began building up.

But once more he pulled back.

"You taste good," he said. "And feel good and smell good."

She said, "Please, for Christ's sake!"

"Sorry."

"Tell me about it later."

She said, "I'm not interested in any more talking."

She took his hand and guided it down to where she wanted him to enter. And kissed him.

And said, "I want you to make love to me. *Now.*"

She kissed him again, this time holding her lips against his, hard, reaching her tongue deep into his mouth, crushing her breasts against his chest, digging her fingers hard into his muscles, until, with the full authority that came from being the one who had set up this arrangement in the first place, rolled over on her back and pulled him onto her. And spread her legs and guided him into where there was the job to be done.

And celebrated the completion of the process with a sharp little cry of pleasure.

It was like being erotically buried under a soft-hard landslide, like creating and controlling an experience that overwhelms you, manipulating its possession of you, turning the wheel upon which you are being turned. And she thrust upward to bring it all closer to her. And cried out at the joy of it.

When he came, the experience was like being part of a train that has chugged and puffed to the top of the hill, then shuddered to a hard and jolting stop, heavy vibrations running from one end to the other and back again and then a final shaking and rocking and the steam escaping and the wheels caving in and the collapse. The wreckage alive and breathing, but inert. And her buried uncomplaining beneath it.

Small sounds. A small final movement. Then nothing.

She felt like asking if he was all right.

After a few long moments he lifted up on his elbows and looked at her. His large hands held her face in a gentle grip.

When he kissed her softly on the lips, she kissed him back.

He said, "Thank you, Maggie."

She felt pregnant already.

"Thank *you,* John."

And she gave his large body a loving squeeze.

She said, "Thank you very much."

11

Toomey raised up on one elbow and looked at the face of the woman lying there. And took a moment to examine it.

The eyebrows were her own, and the eyelids the same color as her soft, smooth cheeks. He liked it that they weren't colored blue or purple. Had they, of course, been colored blue or purple or even with small gold stars pasted on them, he would have loved them that way.

Her hair was black and nothing else.

The forehead was a little higher than is usual. But he liked that. And the white teeth.

She was having nice thoughts about something, apparently. As he watched he saw a small smile come across her lips, and linger there. Then grow.

That was nice. She was happy.

It is good when the woman you've just made love to looks happy. So Toomey, too, smiled.

He still found it hard to believe. And shook his head.
"I don't know," he said. "I don't know."
The soft smile on her face remained. And she didn't open her eyes.
But she asked, "What is it that you don't know, don't know?"
He said, "I don't know what I've done to deserve having something like this happen to me."
He said, "Someone up there must like me. Or feel sorry for me. Or something. And sent you here to make me happy."
The smile stayed on her face, but she opened her eyes.
"I don't know whether anyone up there likes you or not," she said.
"But I know that our being here together is something that I arranged by myself."
She hadn't arranged for his car to break down just where it had, Toomey knew that.
Maybe Madeline Toomey, somewhere out there, had amused herself by giving her namesake this gift of pleasure.
She said, "I liked the way you looked and talked and decided that I wanted to go to bed with you."
She rose up on her elbows and looked over at him and smiled.
"I arranged it all." She bent over and gave him a kiss on the forehead. "And I'm glad that I did. And I thank you once again."
She gave him a final pat on the arm, then sat up and threw the covers off.
He reached out to try to hold on to her, but she was off the bed and onto her feet. And he felt a sudden sinking in his stomach.
"I hope you aren't going."
She stood there, stretching her body, running her fingers through her hair, tossing her head back happily.
"I still owe you lunch."
She stretched once more, raising up on her toes and stretching her arms up toward the ceiling. She held herself that way for

a moment, then came down lightly. And started toward the window.

"I hope you aren't going to leave."

She said, "Not right away."

In front of the window the sunshine outlined her strong figure, laying small shadows between her breasts and below her stomach. The curve of her hips, the firm thighs, and all the individual parts that he had only moments ago held with such delight. And Toomey saw nothing there that was not just as it should be.

"You're very beautiful."

She reached her arms up and rested them on the sides of the window.

"I love sunshine."

Toomey said, "Me too."

She turned from the window and his eyes followed her hopefully as she came back toward the bed. But she didn't lie down again. Instead, she took up her purse, which she had left on the table by the bed, and after a moment found the comb she was looking for.

"I'd like you not to go. I'd at least like to have lunch with you first."

She stood in front of the mirror, now, combing her hair.

"Aren't you going to get out of bed?"

He told her that he would in a minute.

"I enjoy lying here looking at you."

She turned and looked at him, an amused, skeptical expression on her face.

"Sure? Are you sure that you aren't just waiting for me to go to the bathroom so you can get into your clothes?"

But she apologized, quickly, saying, "I'm sorry. I was teasing you."

She moved over and gave him a kiss on the cheek, pulling back in time to avoid the arms he reached out toward her. And turned once more to the mirror and resumed combing her hair.

"But you did seem so shy and modest. I couldn't figure you out."

Toomey said, "I thought that was the way you wanted it. I

realize now that I was wrong."

"The way you got into bed," she said. "As if you were afraid I'd see you naked."

He told her that it was the fault of a woman he'd once known. Thelma something or other.

"She liked to make love in the dark. And from a distance, even, if that were possible."

She took one last pull with the comb, then put it back into her purse.

"You should stay away from people like Thelma," she said. "They're not good for you."

And she looked down at him once more.

"You don't need to be ashamed to let anyone see you naked.

"And you're a very good lover," she added. "Once you get around to it."

A moment later she was over in front of the other window, the one looking out onto the swimming pool and patio.

Toomey was glad to see that she was not making any move toward putting on her clothes.

"I wish you'd come back to bed."

But she shook her head. "I don't want to go back to bed."

Then she said, "But you know what I think I'd like to do?"

"What do you think you'd like to do?"

She said, "I think I'd like to go for a swim."

She reminded him that according to the brochure they had read, there was an indoor pool.

Toomey remembered, unhappily, that he hadn't packed his swimming suit. And told her so.

"I didn't bring mine either," she said. "But I brought a robe."

She looked at him. "Did you bring a robe?"

He had.

"If there is no one in the pool, would it embarrass you to swim without a suit?"

As she turned, the light from the window shifted the shadows on her body, and he took a moment to notice that.

Then he said, "I think I could handle it."

"Would you like to?"

He threw the covers off, said, "Sure," and sat a moment on the edge of the bed, watching her.

"I sure had you figured wrong," he said. And shook his head.

"You're not like Thelma at all."

She said, "Forget about Thelma. Let's have a fast swim, then I've got to go."

They were not surprised to find the pool empty. The noon hour of a weekday during the off season. They changed in the men's dressing room, which was not occupied, and dropped their robes at the edge of the pool.

The pool was not as large as they had expected, but it was adequate. And the water was a little warmer than they would have preferred. But there was a diving board, and that was fun.

After a while a young couple in their early twenties, honeymooners, probably, came to the pool. He let Maggie handle that. She swam, demurely enough, over near where they were and explained that they had forgotten to pack their suits, and did the young couple mind?

They said that they didn't. But they stayed pretty much at their own end of the pool. And left after about only ten or fifteen minutes.

Toomey and Maggie didn't use the diving board while the young people were there.

Toomey asked her once if she often swam in the nude, and she said that she did whenever she had the opportunity.

"Do you?"

He said that he didn't remember swimming in the nude since high school.

They got back to the dressing room to find four men in the process of disrobing. They were all in their early thirties, except for one gray-haired, slender man who was probably in his late forties. They were reviewing a recently completed handball game, apparently, and commenting on how good it had been and how good it was going to be to get into the steam room. But after a glance at who had come into the room, they stopped reviewing and commenting and got very busy untieing shoe laces and taking off their socks.

Maggie took off her robe and threw it on the bench.

Toomey said, "Hi!" and they returned the greeting. Along with the greeting he included a look that meant that he would look unkindly upon anything being said that he didn't approve of.

"That was good," she said, and rubbed the towel hard against her head, then threw her long hair back and shook it.

"I enjoyed that very much."

One of the men said something about how that had been the best workout he'd had for a long time. And the others agreed. Then they gathered up their towels and headed for the showers.

Toomey watched as she finished drying herself. And shook his head again.

He said, "You're really something, Maggie."

She shrugged her shoulders. "No big deal not being afraid to be seen without your clothes on. Though some people would make you think it is."

She said that once she and another woman had desegregated the sauna bath at the Farmington Hilton.

"There was only one sauna, and it was for men only. We didn't like that arrangement."

He asked if she did that kind of thing often, and she said no.

"Some of the women I live with do, though. But there are a lot of things we don't always agree on. Which is all right."

She tossed the towel on the bench and started getting into her clothes. And for a moment they dressed in silence.

Then he looked at her and said, "I think I've fallen in love with you."

And now there was a long, heavy silence. She turned her back and finished dressing.

On the way back she remained silent, and wouldn't look at him. Once he commented that the four men now would have something to tell their friends. And she made no response.

Back in their room, she went to her suitcase, lifted it up and set it on the bed. Then moved over to where her purse was and took out the comb once more.

Toomey said, "I hope you won't go."

She said that she had to. That she hadn't meant to stay this long.

"I'd like to make love to you again."

She said that she had to go. Then finished combing her hair, put the comb back into the purse, and closed it.

"I'd like to very much."

She gave a deep sigh and looked at him, impatiently. And their eyes held for a few moments. Then she sighed once more and said, "All right.

"I guess I owe you that much."

She took her suitcase off the bed and set it again on the floor.

"But I know that I shouldn't."

"If you really don't want to," he said, "it's all right."

That got a nice smile from her. And she held out a hand for him to take.

"No, it's all right."

Then she started laughing. So he joined in.

"But do you mind," she said, "if I go to the bathroom first?"

And she pulled him over to her and they held each other until they'd stopped laughing.

"But I'm not going to get into bed until you come out."

She said, "All right."

That afternoon, with the sunlight flooding the bright room and her dark hair spread across the pillow, Toomey had an experience that he'd never had before. It was very beautiful. And he tried to tell her about it.

He was still holding her face in his hands, lying on top of her, breathing heavily, looking into her eyes.

He said, "It's a feeling I've never known before."

He said, "It's as if I were sending out waves and waves of tenderness, like something pulsating. Radar, or something."

She wasn't happy to be hearing this, as her face showed. She frowned. And the look that came on her face was the one that had been there all the way back from the dressing room.

Her eyes were closed. Her lips tight together.

He kissed them softly, but there was no response.

"I won't say it anymore. I can't really describe it, anyway."

But it was there. That feeling. It emanated from the whole bulk of his body. In a rhythmical pattern, waves and waves of tenderness and kindness and love that flooded out upon her, and he could almost not believe that she couldn't feel it.

But she couldn't, or wouldn't, apparently. She still lay there with her eyes closed. Waiting only for him to get off her.

So he did.

But he said, "Anyway, it's a beautiful feeling. And I thank you for it, Maggie."

He kissed her one last time, then rolled over to his side of the bed, and sat up.

12

Whether it was a characteristic she had got from her mother or from her father, Toni didn't know. But she did know that it was a definite part of her personality that when she said yes she meant yes, and when she said no she meant no.

And she had told John no.

"No. I have to go."

So how come she was sitting in the dining room at the Merritt Inn in the middle of the afternoon having a roast beef sandwich and a glass of beer?

"You are persistent," she said. "I'll say that for you."

He said, "Not always. Only when I have right on my side.

"And you know that it is right that when a woman invites a man to lunch, she actually has lunch with him."

Toni finished the first half of her sandwich, picked up the second half and started on that.

"Okay, so I'm having lunch with you. But it is going to be brief, and then I'm going to be on my way."

He said that he was going to have another beer and did she want one, too, and she said no.

"I have to go. I have things to do."

She hoped that hadn't sounded hard or critical. As if he, too, should have something better to do than sit around all afternoon drinking beer.

She was being uptight again. And told herself to relax.

"But you stay and enjoy yourself. After all, you're on vacation."

He succeeded in getting the attention of the waitress. Held up the empty bottle and one finger.

"I have a child I must get back to."

That seemed to please him. She saw a quick smile come to his face.

He said, "That's nice."

"People are taking care of her for me, of course." She wanted him to know that.

You could see that he was about to ask how old the child was, and things like that, so she said quickly, "But I really don't want to talk about it."

He was disappointed. But he said, "All right."

And for a few moments they ate in silence.

The waitress came with his beer.

After she had gone, he said, "I've decided to change my name. I don't like John. It's too biblical."

She almost told him that she didn't care what he changed it to, but then got very sharp with herself. He was trying to get back some of the lightness of their morning talk, and she was at the point of being rude.

He was, after all, the father of the child she was going to have. The least she could do was to be reasonably pleasant during their last few minutes together.

She asked, "Would you like George? I've always rather liked that name."

He said that if that was what she liked, then that was what it would be.

She said that she was satisfied with the name Maggie. But not Brown.

"If it's not too late, I think I'll change that."

He said that he thought something Irish would be good. And she said she thought so, too.

"One of my parents is Irish."

"Don't tell me which one," he said. And they laughed.

He suggested O'Reilly.

"Then you could use that old vaudeville joke. Where you say that you are half Irish and the other person says, 'Oh, really?' and you say, 'No. O'Reilly'!"

She liked that. So he said he'd go tell the desk clerk that they had changed their names. Right after they had finished lunch.

So this was nice. Fun again, like this morning. A nice way to end what had been an enjoyable experience.

She wiped her mouth with the napkin and pushed her plate half an inch away, which is the international signal that you have finished.

She said, "That was good. I'm glad you talked me into it. But now I've got to go."

He said, "Was it because of what I said in the dressing room? That I thought I had fallen in love with you?"

He was looking at her, unsmiling. Very serious.

"Was it?"

She didn't want to talk about it. But he persisted.

"Was it?"

"What difference does it make?"

"Was it?"

All right. She agreed that it was.

"Why did that make you angry?"

She felt the anger returning.

"Because that was not part of the arrangement. That's why."

She said, "It was as if you were giving me your opinion on something that was none of your business."

He didn't agree with that. He said, "I think it is very much my business how I feel about someone."

She said, "Okay, it's not that it was none of your business. It was just that it had nothing to do with the situation."

"What was the situation?"

"The situation was simply that we met by chance along the road, and that I liked the way you looked and talked and I wanted to go to bed with you.

"And did. And enjoyed myself.

"And now I'm going to be getting on my way."

Putting it that way made her seem like something she wasn't, really. And she expected to see a look of disapproval or disappointment on his face.

But instead the smile came through again.

"Maggie, you're really something! You really are."

He finished his sandwich, brushed the napkin across his mouth, pushed his plate the prescribed half inch, then had a long drink of his beer.

"I will always remember that you said you enjoyed it. That I pleased you for part of a day.

"That will be a nice memory," he said. And poured the rest of his beer into the glass.

"Now you get on your way any time you're ready," he said. "I don't want to keep you from whatever it is that you have to do."

He looked in the direction of the waitress.

"As for myself, I think I'll stay here and have just one more beer before I get back on the road."

He wouldn't have just one more, she knew that. He'd have half a dozen. And sit here feeling sorry for himself. And that made her angry.

She said, "Look, John, let me tell you something."

"George."

"George, then. Just let me explain something to you for your own damn good."

He seemed willing to listen, so she continued.

"You don't know anything at all about me. Where I came from, what I am. So when you tell me that you love me, all you're saying, really, is that you are ready to fall in love with the first woman who will be nice to you."

He was still trying to get the waitress's attention.

She said, "That will get you into a lot of trouble."

"Sure you don't want another beer?"

"No."

She said, "You go around telling women that you love them and you will find yourself in serious trouble."

He said, "I got an idea."

"Somewhere tonight you're going to stop at a bar somewhere between here and the cape, and you'll find a woman who'll let you buy her a drink. And she'll listen to your troubles and hold your dumb head and take you home with her. And unless she does something outrageous, like spitting on the floor, by morning you'll have agreed to take care of her and her family for the rest of their lives."

"What's wrong with spitting on the floor?"

All right. So they both laughed a bit about that. But she felt she had made her point.

He said, "I got this idea."

"It's probably dumb."

"Actually," he said, "it's not."

She shouldn't wait around to hear what it was. She knew that. She should just get up and go.

"What is it?"

First, he said that he tended to agree with her that he wasn't very bright as far as women were concerned. Maybe he hadn't really fallen in love with her. Even though he felt quite sure that he had.

"Sometimes we think we are more in love than we really are."

She said, "Go ahead."

"On the other hand," he said, "sometimes we meet someone and later, when we think back on it, wish we'd got to know them better and had got their phone number or address or by some means had learned how to get in touch with that person again."

His point was simple enough. If they parted too hastily, he said, one or the other might regret it.

He glanced at his watch. "Believe it or not, it's only three-thirty. Since we met at ten o'clock this morning, we've had a drink, made love, gone for a swim, made love again, and had lunch."

"So?"

"So, I suggest we separate for a while. I will get my bag and put it in the car and go for a ride, and think about it. And you do the same."

"I knew that it would be a dumb idea."

"Even better, of course, would be for us to go together to some quiet place, by the side of a lake somewhere, and talk about it. Or go have dinner somewhere. And then, at the end of the evening, if you have decided that you don't want to see me again, I'll get in my car and go."

She said, "If I had to choose, I think the first would be better than the second."

He said, "All right." And outlined the plan.

"We both go for a ride and think about it. If either of us feels that it would be better not to see the other again, he or she just keeps going. And if either of us feels that we would like to see the other again, we come back here and take a table and wait to see if the other shows up."

Toni said, "Don't tell me which table."

He changed his mind. "We meet at the bar, not here. It will be too crowded here. We might miss each other."

He asked, "All right?"

After a moment she said, "All right."

"You will think it over? Not just get into your car and drive away?"

She said she'd think it over.

"If either of us is interested in seeing the other person, he or she is back at the bar by five o'clock."

"I understand the arrangement, George. But I won't be here at five o'clock."

He said that maybe he wouldn't be there either.

"I'm going to go somewhere and think very seriously about what you've said. It may well be that you are right. And maybe it's time that I woke up. Before I get into more trouble."

"If either of us does decide to come back," Toni said, "that would not commit either of us to anything more than simply having dinner together."

"Of course not."

He asked if she'd like another beer before they left, and she said no.

"Five o'clock, then."

"Five o'clock. But I won't be here."

"Do you want to go first?"

"No. You go first. I'll stay here and have another cup of coffee."

She reached out and took the check. "And I'll pay for this."

As he stood up, she said, "When I get out to the parking lot I'd better not see your car there."

He said, "You won't."

He reached down his hand and she took it.

He said, "Maggie, if for some reason I don't see you again, I want to thank you for one of the happiest days of my life."

She said, "Just go, will you?"

"I'm going." And he released her hand.

Toni watched the big man make his way across the room, weaving around and between the tables, giving a small wave and a smile, probably, to the waitress as he passed.

And about the time he got near the door, she gave in.

All right, when he turned for that last look back, she'd wave to him to return to the table and they'd talk about it some more. Maybe talking about it over dinner would be better, after all.

But he went out the door without looking back.

That was too bad.

13

Toomey and Myra had another game that didn't take much skill or concentration. They played it this morning while he was writing checks and paying bills and she was busy putting little colored pegs into a board with holes in it.

He said, "If this stack of bills gets any higher it'll fall over and land on my *head!*" And he laughed.

She scanned the board to see which small hole could use a little green peg in it. Selected one, finally, and without looking up, said, "If that stack of bills gets any higher it will fall over and land on your *nose!*" And she laughed.

Roman thumped his tail. That was his small contribution to the game.

Toomey stuffed a check into an envelope, licked the flap, wiped his tongue on the sleeve of his shirt, and said, "If that stack of bills gets any higher it will fall over and land on my *ear!*" And this time they both laughed.

She took a few moments deciding just which color peg she wanted to use next, finally selected an orange one, and said, "If that stack of bills gets any higher it will fall over and land on your *big toe!*" And this time they both laughed a little louder and a little longer.

The purpose of this game is to see if you can each time increase the loudness and the duration of the laughs that follow the part of the anatomy referred to. By the time one or the other got around to predicting that it might fall and land on his *belly button,* people passing on the sidewalk would stop and look at one another and wonder just what the hell was going on with Toomey and his bunch of crazy women.

Toomey got a phone call from Diana Morgenthau. She was the social worker who had come here a month ago and talked him into hiring Glenna. Diana had explained that she wasn't officially Glenna's social worker any longer, because Glenna had left her care when she became eighteen. But she was still interested in the girl's welfare and was trying to help her. From the way she had described Glenna at the time, Toomey had told her that he knew she wouldn't work out. But she had talked him into giving the girl a chance anyway.

"Glenna tells me that you are going to fire her."

Toomey said that he hadn't heard that.

"Well, are you?"

"She didn't come in today," Toomey said. "But if she comes in tomorrow and says she wants to keep on working, she can."

"She says that you don't like her."

Toomey thought about that for a moment. Then said, "She's probably right. Though that doesn't mean that I wouldn't let her work here."

"The girl's had a rough life," Ms. Morgenthau said. "I think the least you could do is encourage her."

"I tried to," Toomey said. "I encouraged her to say something nice about someone sometime just to see what her reaction would be. But she wouldn't try it."

"Is that your idea of how to help someone?"

Toomey said, "Yes. Part of it." And there was a long pause on both ends of the line.

Toomey finally said, "I'd like to praise her for her good qualities, but I haven't spotted any."

A moment later he asked, "Did you spot any?"

She said, "Glenna's had a very difficult life. She has a very low image of herself."

"That's not a good quality."

"I'm not saying it's a good quality. I'm saying that it's a fact. Just like it's a fact that her mother is an alcoholic and her father doesn't work. The family's been on welfare for years."

"Doesn't sound like good qualities run in her family," Toomey said. "Maybe we should encourage her to develop some of her own.

"Like speaking to Mrs. Murphey with a little respect," he said. "Doing a good job at whatever she's doing."

Nothing from the other end of the line.

"So unless you got a better idea, let's start with encouraging her to do or say a loving thing for someone. Maybe they'll do or say something nice back and she'll like that. And try it again. The whole thing may snowball and she'll be so busy doing nice things and having nice things done to her in return that she won't need your help anymore."

Since she was still not saying anything, Toomey kept on a little longer.

"If she complains to you that people don't like her, tell her that it's only because she's unlikeable. Nothing incurable. Nothing she can't change. Suggest she give other people a little consideration. And tell her that if she wants to develop a better image of herself, all she has to do is do some things that make her proud of herself."

He didn't know if she was still on the line or not, but before he hung up he said, "Anyway, one thing I insist on is that if she wants to work here she has to act decently to her boss, Mrs. Murphey."

"It hurts me," she said, "to think that you have a lot of impressionistic young women working for you. Young women who need sympathy and understanding."

She said, "I wish there were something I could do to put you out of business."

"You'd have to get in line," Toomey said. "Lots of other

people are ahead of you."

But the conversation now was becoming tiresome and a bit silly. So Toomey said, "Anyway, tell her to come back to work if she wants to. Under the conditions I laid down. Or else come in and pick up her check."

"I'll find her a job somewhere else."

Toomey said, "All right." But then he remembered.

"She won't be there very long, unfortunately. Because this fall, at a carnival or fair or something in Farmington, she's going to get involved with one of the workers who'll get her drugged or drunk or something and take her along with them when the carnival leaves town."

He said, "Farmington does have a carnival or fair or something in the fall, doesn't it?"

She said, "Every place has a carnival or fair or something in the fall."

"Probably," Toomey agreed. "But remember that I made that prediction. That one of the carnival workers would get her drugged or drunk and carry her off when they leave town."

He told her to write it down on her calendar.

He had barely finished talking with Diana Morgenthau when he got a call from Chief Nicocci, who told him that Mrs. Boughton was complaining again about the noise of motorcycles in front of Toomey's place at closing time.

"She said that a couple nights ago it was so bad that it gave her a headache."

"I wasn't here that afternoon," Toomey said. "I was in Boston."

"Then you probably couldn't hear it," Nick said. "You probably couldn't hear it any farther away than Springfield."

That wasn't bad, and Toomey laughed.

He said, "Now that you mention it, Nick, I think I did hear a little something at about that time. But I only thought it was some trucks backfiring."

Nick was not one of those who were trying to run Toomey out of town. He had, in fact, been friendly. One Sunday morning at Harvey's, where everyone goes for the Sunday paper, Toomey ran into Nick and got fifteen minutes' worth of good advice on bass fishing in and around Munsen. Nick told him that you don't get the big ones on minnows or worms and that you have to use surface lures like the Hula popper or the Crazy Crawler and fish in and around the lily pads at sunset. Toomey had got one of each from Harvey, and Nick had even helped him pick them out.

"Why don't you arrest them for disturbing the peace?" Toomey said.

He added, "Have George Greenly throw the handcuffs on all of them some afternoon."

George Greenly was a policeman in town who was fast with the handcuffs. He loved arresting people. Especially young people. Toomey had never met him—Greenly apparently either not getting a Sunday paper or else sending his wife or someone else in to pick it up—but it had so happened that the very first week Toomey opened up the business, one of his employees, a young woman named Elva Feldman, had happened to hit Greenly's hunting dog. She was driving down Burton Road in her little Volkswagen and the dog had run in front of her car, right in front of the Greenly house. The dog wasn't hurt bad, but Greenly was pretty mad.

Only a few minutes before, Elva had been smoking some grass with a friend in the car after work, and when Greenly had gone over to the car to check out her registration and license, he had smelled the odor of marijuana and had searched the car and gone through her pockets and had got madder and madder when he couldn't find anything. He'd had his handcuffs handy and could have thrown them on her right there beside the road. Right in front of the wife and kids.

Elva moved on to another job a few weeks later and the incident was forgotten. But word was out around town that Greenly was disgusted because Nicocci wouldn't let him walk right into Baskets and Baskets and search the place from top to bottom and throw handcuffs on everyone there.

"You've got to handle it," Nick said. "Or else she's going to take her complaint to the town selectmen." And he said that if the selectmen got too many complaints they could cause a lot of trouble.

That made sense, so Toomey said, "Thanks for calling me about it."

He promised that he would deal with the situation the next time the kids showed up.

He went back to writing checks and paying bills.

Taking a bill from the top of the pile, he said to Myra, "If my problems pile up any higher they'll all come crashing down on my *Adam's apple.*"

They both laughed so long and loud that the women working in the next room looked at one another and shook their heads.

Mrs. Murphey said, "It's too bad he never had children. He's so good with them."

The young men on motorcycles arrived a few minutes before five.

There were three of them. They came roaring in from the north, then swung around and parked at the curb in front of the building and took turns revving up their motors. The noise they made was not only loud, but had a deliberate, taunting, insulting quality about it. You could picture Mrs. Boughton across the street shaking her head, putting her hands over her ears, and heading for the telephone.

Toomey left the baseball bat inside. And made Roman stay inside, too.

He said, "I'll handle this."

The three motorcyclists hadn't dressed up or put on their best manners for the occasion. All had long hair, dark beards, and ugly expressions. Toomey had nothing against long hair, beards, or unattractive facial features—himself not being the best-looking man on the block—but these lads were making a point of looking frightening. Their bikes were huge complexes of chrome and steel, and behind the seats were black pouches which no doubt held bombs and machine guns and three pounds of pure heroin.

Toomey laughed. Why, or at what, he wasn't quite sure.

He said, "Hey, friends. Turn off your motors a minute."

They didn't do so right away. But they offered the temporary courtesy of not revving their engines.

Toomey wasn't satisfied with that. He said, "You'll have to turn them off. I need to talk to you and I don't want to have to shout."

Toomey didn't know anything about motorcycles, but these looked to be unnecessarily big and overloaded with gadgets. One had a jagged metal bar perpendicular to a rear support, which didn't seem to serve any obvious purpose that he could see.

All of them wore black jackets. Two were over six feet, heavy, and looked much alike. Long blond hair that showed below the hard black helmets. Probably brothers. The one in the middle wasn't quite as tall, leaner, with a red scar that slanted across his right cheek. He had the angry expression of one who was capable of doing at any moment anything he damned well felt like doing and worrying about the consequences sometime later. Like maybe year after next.

Toomey reminded himself that there are all kinds of kids who ride bikes. And that you can't judge people by their appearance, and that someone picking up his girl friend after work can't be all bad.

Finally, one of the tall ones shut off his bike and got off. He took off his helmet and hung it on the handlebar. And moved a few feet to one side.

The one on the other end, the other brother, turned off his engine but didn't get off the bike. And he, too, hung his helmet on the handlebar. And looked at Toomey.

"First," Toomey said, "Glenna didn't come to work today. So she isn't here to be picked up."

He got the impression, from the looks on their faces, that they already knew that.

"More important," he said, "there's an old lady across the street whose nerves aren't as good as they used to be. She can't stand the noise. So I've got to ask you to pick up Glenna somewhere down the street a ways. Or else somehow manage to come and go without making so much noise."

For some reason Toomey assumed that the one with his motor still running, the one in the middle, was Cruiser, Glenna's boyfriend. So he addressed his remarks to that one.

"I'm Toomey Bougereau. I run this place."

The young man wasn't impressed. And showed it. But Toomey tried not to let that bother him.

"I don't mind your picking up Glenna and I don't mind your riding your bikes here to do it. But what I'm asking you to do, as a favor to all of us, is pick her up at the corner, down by the gas station."

No one said anything, so he asked again.

"How about it?"

The young man didn't answer with words. His mouth twisted into a challenging grin, and he gunned the motor hard with a blast that hurt Toomey's ears and seemed almost to make the ground shake.

Once in high school when the Wildcats were playing Thompson High School in Westfield, while untangling from a pileup the Thompson quarterback had deliberately and maliciously kicked Toomey in the face. Out of pure meanness, as far as anyone could see. Toomey had tackled him cleanly, almost gently. Just stopping him.

It was the only time Toomey had got kicked out of a game.

He had grabbed that boy and pulled him to his feet and had then thrown him back on the ground so hard that his friends told him you could hear the impact up in the stands. But what was most interesting was that later he remembered that it had all happened and was over with before he was consciously aware that he was actually doing it.

It was that way this time.

Toomey grabbed the kid by the lapels of his jacket and yanked him off the bike and threw him across the sidewalk and onto the grass, picked him up and spun him around and grabbed his wrists and twisted both arms behind him.

Then he backed up until he was almost against the building.

And now was aware of what he had done and was doing.

He twisted the kid's arms up higher and said, "Tell them to stay where they are or I'll break both your goddamn arms."

And when the kid twisted and tried to pull away, Toomey pulled the arms up farther and gave him a knee hard in the small of the back.

The other two were coming at him and Toomey yelled at them to stay back.

"I said tell them to hold up." And he twisted a little tighter until the kid got the words out.

He said, "Hold up." And they did.

And for a moment there was silence except for Toomey's heavy breathing and the sound of Roman trying to tear the door down.

One of the two pulled something from his jacket pocket and held it in his fist. The other moved around to Toomey's other side.

"I'm going to count three," Toomey said, "then I start breaking."

And he said, "One."

The two shifted around a bit and circled some but didn't come any closer.

"Two," Toomey said. And the boy gave a small scream.

Then the two moved back. So Toomey eased up a bit.

Apparently the women in the shop had gathered behind the bay window in the shop and were watching. One of them screamed. And Roman was throwing himself against the glass.

It was time to end this and Toomey told the boy that.

"If they don't get moving out of here right now, you're going to lose the use of your arms for a long, long time."

And he started the pressure.

The kid cursed his friends and told them to go.

And Toomey eased up.

The two turned, and without looking back, went to their bikes, started the motors, and, still not looking back, roared off.

Toomey turned the kid loose and followed him back to his bike.

"I'm sorry I had to hurt you."

127

There was no response to that.

The boy put on the helmet and got onto the seat. He still hadn't looked at Toomey or said anything.

But just as he pulled away he threw a parting comment over his shoulder.

And the way he phrased it was, "You goddamn fuckin' son of a bitch! I'll get you for this."

14

One of the people who thought that Munsen, Massachusetts, would be better off without Toomey Bougereau was Mrs. Walter Carew. She went out of her way to share this viewpoint with everyone who was willing to listen, and after a while she became more or less the official spokesman for the people who thought the Crandalls should be talked into coming out of retirement and return once again to operate the Munsen Roadside Gift Shop.

Those had been the good days. When the only creatures running around town with long hair and bare feet were Tom Porter's two sheep dogs. And when you could walk down Main Street at noon and not see a lot of half-dressed young women playing Frisbee on the grass. Or maybe walking down from Baskets and Baskets to Harvey's for cigarettes and the chance to show off their bare stomachs.

Back in February, less than two months after Toomey had

started his business, Mrs. Carew had gone there to apply for work. She didn't really want a job, since she had a large house and three children to take care of, but she wanted to investigate the rumor that you couldn't get a job at Baskets and Baskets unless you were young and sexy.

Mrs. Carew was fifty years old and already two generations removed from her teen-age and young-adult children. She was very heavy, talked in a loud voice, and was known for taking extreme positions on what ordinarily are noncontroversial subjects. She blamed the schools for the fact that she could no longer relate to her children. And to see that this didn't happen to other parents, she was the leader of a small and informal group of parents who kept a close and critical eye on the kinds of books the local grade school and the regional high school exposed their children to.

She said that you should see the kind of books they have in the libraries and classrooms of the schools these days.

No wonder parents have lost control of their children.

Mrs. Carew had gone to see Mr. Bougereau one Monday morning during the last week of the month. She remembered that it was about eleven in the morning. But even that early in the day, he'd been drinking. You could tell. On his desk was a small paper cup that you could be pretty sure was filled with whiskey.

And he looked tired. As if he'd been out all night the night before.

She said that he had thanked her for coming in, but told her that in addition to Mrs. Murphey, he had four girls working for him at the present time.

"And that's as many as I can use."

That was a brazen, though honest, way of putting it. And she scowled at him.

"You can't use more than four?"

He said no. And shook his head.

"And none of them is planning to leave. Far as I know."

Mrs. Carew said, "I happen to know that several people have quit already. And you've been in business less than two months."

Toomey explained that this is the kind of job that gets boring in a very short time.

"Weaving baskets, mostly the same kind over and over, is not the most exciting way to spend the day."

Mrs. Carew gave him her unsmiling, appraising look. The kind that makes it clear that she is not the kind of person to be easily fooled.

"I'd like to leave my application."

He had smiled and said, "I've not got into the habit of keeping applications, Mrs. Carew." He had gestured toward a cardboard box at one end of the desk. "I keep a minimum of records."

She could believe that. He certainly didn't look like much of a businessman. She could easily believe that in that one box was all the records the company had. It was at times like this that she wished that for just one day she could be working for the Internal Revenue Service and come in and ask to look at his records.

But what had struck her most forcibly, as she had told her husband that night at dinner, was what Mr. Bougereau had done to that beautiful building that the Crandalls had kept so immaculately clean and attractive.

In that large room with the beautiful bay window, where there had been those many tables and shelves stocked with lovely gifts and greeting cards, there were now large coils of whatever it is they make baskets out of, workers walking on it, kicking it aside, no doubt breaking and wasting it. Scraps of lumber all over the place. Someone was sawing wood at a table and kicking sawdust around until the air was filled with it. The place looked like a barn, she said. And there was loud rock and roll music coming from a radio. At one end of the room was a sink that probably had not been cleaned since the Crandalls had left. Windows so dirty you could hardly see out of them.

"Just the sight of it," she said, "was enough to make me almost cry."

When she said to him that she'd come in some other time to see if he needed anyone, he had discouraged her.

He had told her that he didn't think she'd be happy there.

"Except for Mrs. Murphey," he said, "the women out there are all very young. They like to play loud music of the kind that would drive you out of your mind. They talk all day long about things that I know would irritate you. Where they've been and

131

what they've done, their boyfriends, sex. And how dumb people over thirty are."

That, in her opinion, had been his way of saying that she wasn't young and sexy enough.

She asked if he ever hired married women, and he said no. He preferred young and unmarried women who were sort of temporarily down on their luck and needed to pick up a little money to get them through whatever little emergency they were going through.

She said, bluntly, "I can guess why."

She told her husband that it makes a person sick to her stomach to think of what goes on in places like that. Young women who know that if they are going to keep their jobs they've got to do whatever the boss wants them to do. And she tried to brush from her mind pictures of him doing the kinds of things to those girls that she knew he'd want to do.

She had said, "You look tired."

He said that he hadn't slept well the night before.

"Business problems?"

He said no. He'd lain awake most of the night thinking about a woman he had loved very much. And lost.

"I hear that you've been married twice."

He had admitted that that was true.

She caught him glancing over at his paper cup.

"Have you been drinking?"

He said, "Matter of fact, I have." And he reached out, took the paper cup, and took a sip from it.

"Would you like a little?"

When she told that to her husband, he said, "That son of a bitch!"

"Then I told him that I thought he was a disgrace to the community and that I thought his place of business should be closed down. And that what he was doing to the helpless young women there was criminal and that he should be ashamed of himself."

"What did he say to that?"

"He said that I sounded now like I really did need a drink. And he got a bottle of whiskey out of the desk, filled the cup, and held it out to me."

"That bastard!"

As Walt Carew knew very well, you can't, of course, get a man chased out of town just because he happens to be having a little drink in his office and offers some to your wife. But you don't have to take that kind of thing sitting down, either.

There is always something you can do.

If you happen to work for the town highway department and you drive a snowplow, you can always manage to push a little more snow into a man's driveway than usual. And if you are lucky enough to have a real heavy snow, as they happened to have in Munsen that March, you can push the snow quite a ways in. Especially if you're working at four o'clock in the morning and there's no one there to see you, you can go across the street in front of Mrs. Boughton's place and push snow from there across the street and straight into the driveway.

A photographer from the *Farmington Courier* even came down to Munsen for a picture of how high the snow had drifted on the north side of Main Street in front of Baskets and Baskets. And while he was there he took pictures of the girls at noontime throwing snowballs in front of the building and posing beside the snowman they'd built.

It turned out that the *Courrier* printed pictures of the girls rather than of the high snowdrifts.

Which, according to Mrs. Carew, is a fine commentary on the way the world is today. When the newspaper finds nothing more attractive in the whole town of Munsen than long-haired girls in dungarees and tight sweaters.

But that was last winter. Now it was early August and people were complaining about the heat, not the snow.

Toomey had just got back to the office after taking Roman and Myra for a walk down at Harvey's. One for the exercise and the other for a chocolate ice-cream cone.

The phone rang as he came through the door.

He picked up the phone, said hello, and heard a young woman's voice say, "Oh! That's too bad." And wondered what had happened.

He said, "I'm sorry. What's wrong?"

"If you had answered the phone with 'I love WFRM radio' you'd have won a prize."

Toomey said, "Damn!"

Then he said, "I wasn't thinking. My mind was on something else."

"That's too bad."

He asked if she'd give him another chance. He'd hang up and she could call him right back.

But she said that that would be against the rules. And she apologized once more and said that she hoped he wasn't too disappointed.

"Well, some," he admitted. "But I don't want you to feel bad. It's not your fault."

He said, "You sound like a nice person. The next time you're in Munsen, stop in at Baskets and Baskets and if you say the magic word, which is 'Hello,' you win a free can of cold soda."

She said she'd remember that, and that she'd ask her supervisor if it would be all right to call him back, but she was pretty sure she wouldn't be allowed to.

Anyway, they agreed that it had been nice meeting each other, and they hung up.

The phone did ring about a minute later, but it wasn't her.

Toomey said, "I love WFRM radio," and after a moment an older woman's voice said, "Is this Mr. Toomey Bougereau?"

She had a little trouble with both the first and the second name, as if she didn't quite believe either to be real, but Toomey admitted right away that she had the right party and she said, "Hold the phone, please. Judge Lanahan would like to speak to you."

Judge Lanahan. That would be Angela's father.

While he waited, Toomey got a mental picture of what the man probably looked like. Tall, dignified, and sober. A strong profile, with a little gray in the hair. And a voice that rang of the oratory of ancient Rome. Or Greece. Pericles, maybe.

When his honor finally got to the phone, the voice turned out to be rather thin, high pitched, hesitant. The revised picture was of someone thin, slender, rimless glasses, light brown hair, and not very much of that, even.

"I wonder what you could tell me about my daughter."

Toomey had to think about that for a moment. You can't just tell a man that his adoptive daughter is quite possibly at this moment in a motel room somewhere in New Jersey providing sexual satisfaction for some middle-aged traveling salesman.

"What was it you wanted to know, Judge?"

"Do you know where she is?"

"Not exactly," Toomey said. "But I have the feeling that she is somewhere in New Jersey."

"Have you heard from her?"

"No. But I expect to, any day now."

Toomey said, "She has, her friends tell me, a pattern of taking off every once in a while. For a week or two. Gets everybody worried about her. Then she comes home with a rush, apologizes for worrying everyone, gets a big hugging, a happy welcome back."

He said, "It's her way of getting reassurance that people still care for her."

"Are you sure that that is what happened this time?"

Toomey said that he could only assume that that is what had happened. Hard to be sure of anything.

"Her mother and I are very worried about her."

"I'm sure you are. I'm sorry she does this to you."

There was silence for a moment or two, then the judge said, "We've tried to find out why she does it. We've spared no expense to get the best advice possible."

"Sometimes the best advice available isn't much good," Toomey said.

"I know."

"One thing you might do," Toomey said, "when you hear from her, is make sure she understands that you want her home. She thinks you don't want her home because her problems embarrass you and your wife and that you want to send her away to sort of get her out of sight. As it were."

"That isn't true," the judge said. "I mean it isn't true that we think that. Although it is probably true, as you say, that that is what she thinks."

Then the judge, with the ring of sincerity in his voice, said that he wanted Toomey to know that he did not agree with and was not supporting the stand taken by Reverend Osterman.

"What stand is that?"

"The reverend thinks that the girl was encouraged to commit suicide by your telling her that it was all right to do so."

"Is that so?"

"He plans to ask the police to go around and talk to you. Maybe get volunteers to search the woods in the area."

Then he said, "Hold on a moment." And there was silence for half a minute or more.

Then, "Look. I've got to go. But I'll be talking with you again."

"Okay," Toomey said. "And don't worry about anything."

And they both said good-bye and hung up.

Mrs. Murphey came in with a young woman who was looking for work. She reminded Toomey that with Glenna probably not coming back and with Angela gone, they were shorthanded.

The woman's name was Sarah Weinert. She was twenty-six years old. She needed a job very much in order to get enough money together to get her two children and herself to Austin, Texas, where she had a brother who could help her find a permanent job.

Toomey asked her a few pertinent questions, like did she smoke grass and run over people's dogs and did she have a boyfriend who piloted a helicopter who'd want to pick her up after work.

She said that she didn't use drugs and didn't have a driver's license and was afraid to fly. So Toomey asked Mrs. Murphey to introduce her to the other workers and show her how to do the job. And he wished her good luck.

She wished him good luck, too. And he said thanks.

Later in the day, Glenna came in to pick up her check.

Toomey told her that Ms. Morgenthau had called, and she made a sour face to show what she thought of Ms. Morgenthau.

"She's trying to help you," Toomey said.

Glenna made the face again, and repeated what she'd said a

moment ago. That she'd come in to pick up her check.

"She thinks that I'm being unfair to you by not taking into consideration the fact that you have problems at home."

He said, "I'd like to talk to you about it. If you want, I'd even go around and talk to your parents about it."

"Are you going to pay me my money, or not?"

Toomey sighed, said, "Okay," and reached into the drawer for the checkbook.

"If you want to come back to work, you can, you know. All you have to do is promise to try to be better to Mrs. Murphey."

She said, "All I want is my money. You owe me for two full days."

While he was making out the check, she said, "And you might as well know, the Hornets are going to get you."

He said, "All right."

"You don't nearly cripple one of their gang and get away with it."

He said, "They'll need more than just the three of them."

"They got more," Glenna said. "They got all they need."

He gave her a check for three days' work.

"Good luck to you."

She got halfway to the door before he remembered.

"Glenna?"

She stopped and turned around.

"Stay away from the carnival this fall."

Her only answer was to slam the door on the way out.

Later, while Myra was having her nap, Toomey went into the shop to see how things were going and to make a few baskets.

The new girl seemed to be catching on quickly, which was good. Mrs. Murphey said that she was catching on quicker than anyone they had ever had before.

And no one's eardrums had got busted yet from the volume of the rock music coming out of the radio. He was glad of that, Toomey said, because his insurance didn't cover busted eardrums resulting from the radio being turned up too high. But as a further precaution, just to be safe, he wondered if maybe they should turn it down even more. Mrs. Murphey suggested they turn it all the way off, but that was voted down. As a compromise they left it on but only at a volume that shook the windows no more than once every minute or two.

He found that he had interrupted Sarah's telling of her life story.

It seems to be customary for all new workers to do that when they first come to work. That is the part of the orientation program that follows immediately after the brief period of instruction on how to weave a basket.

Toomey had missed the part where she had dropped out of high school, worked at the check-out counter of the A & P, and had had two children. A boy and a girl. She hadn't been married to the father of the boy but he had deserted her anyway. Then she had married his best friend, who was the father of her three-year-old girl.

Sarah picked up the story where she had left off.

Her husband, Frank, was in jail for armed robbery. And this was not his first time there. He loved guns and fast cars, and robbery was the only kind of work he cared for. And although she loved him, in a way, she was going to get a divorce because she was tired of his being away from home so much, sometimes for sixty or ninety days at a stretch.

She and her two children were staying with her sister here in Munsen. She didn't plan to work here more than a few weeks, just long enough to be able to get money for a bus ticket to Austin, Texas. Where her brother was.

She'd like to visit her husband, but he was mad at her because he'd heard that she was running around with other men while he was in jail. Which wasn't true. But she knew that her husband was on work detail away from the jail during the day and she was scared to death that he'd get hold of a gun and come looking for her.

She kept coming back to that one particular fear. How afraid she was that he might escape and get a gun, somehow, and come looking for her and whoever it was he thought she might be running around with. She said he was probably the most jealous person she had ever known.

Mrs. Murphey asked if her husband knew where she was living, and Sarah said yes.

"And he'll find out where I'm working, too," she said. "I don't know how he will find out. But he will."

And she looked out the window toward the street.

Everyone else looked out the window toward the street, too.

15

Toomey realized that it made no sense to walk out of the restaurant without looking back to see if maybe Maggie had changed her mind. But that is what he did. Waved at the waitress, didn't look back, and went out the door.

Once he'd turned the corner, however, he stopped. And debated whether to go back in and see if she agreed with him that this was silly. This coming and going. Leaving and returning. And it was at least half a minute that he stood there before reluctantly continuing on his way.

He had said that he would do it, so he did. Toomey went back to his room and got his bag. It was a gesture that he knew was unnecessary, but an agreement must be honored. As agreed, they would have this interlude, this period of time when he went away and pretended to have to decide whether or not to come back.

As if the decision could possibly be in doubt.

Of course he would come back.

And so would she. He knew that. Though nothing she had said had indicated that she would. She had even tried to give the impression that she wouldn't.

But Toomey was almost thirty-eight years old. And when you get that old and you've played a little poker and done some bass fishing you know very well when the game has turned in your favor. When the outcome is certain and all you have to do is to sit back and play it right.

There are some times, of course, when you've got a big one on the line and because of the way it's fighting and because of the particular place on the lake you are in, you can't be really sure that you'll get it into the boat, regardless of how well you play it. But other times, after only a few seconds, you know for sure that it's only a matter of time.

You might as well start warming up the frying pan.

He thought of Madeline Toomey and wondered if she'd ever have been able to predict that her namesake would finally stumble upon happiness in this strange way and this far from Angora, Indiana.

Before he left the room he stood for a while by the window and looked toward the faraway hills and thought about it.

You wonder sometimes if something like this could ever happen just by chance. Or is it more likely that someone is somewhere manipulating some strings to cause to be brought together in such unusual circumstances two people so obviously made for each other?

He had the feeling that when she did finally tell him about herself, he would not be surprised. The Madeline Toomey influence once more. The ability to guess with a high degree of accuracy what the person had been like earlier, and what the future was going to bring.

He would guess that she had once been a nun. Or something like that. Had lived in a convent or some other protected environment until she was twenty-five or so. Then had reversed her feelings completely, had lived a rather wild life for a while—the

142

other extreme—and had now settled somewhere in between. Probably worked in the office at a Catholic grammar school. Or as a librarian.

During her wild years she had had a child. The result of a romantic fling, a joyous and exuberant entrance into the real world of sensual pleasure. And tonight sometime she'd tell him about it and about the child.

She was no doubt a good mother and the child was beautiful. He and the child would be good friends. Play games and do things together.

He left the key at the desk and when the clerk asked if he was checking out, he said no. He said he'd be back.

He put the bag into the car, got the screwdriver out of the glove compartment, and, with no trouble, started the car. And was pleased with himself at the pleasure he got from that simple mechanical act. The screwdriver across the terminal points. A child could do it. Once someone had shown it how.

The reason we feel so much at the mercy of these mechanical contrivances is that we know so little about them. We limit ourselves to what the instructions tell us.

Turn this key clockwise and put your right foot on that pedal. And it will start. Simple enough. But when it doesn't start, then we don't know what to do.

Someday, Toomey promised himself, he'd take time to learn something about automobiles.

He rested the screwdriver on the fender and did things like check the water in the radiator and in the battery. You can't check the oil when the motor is running—he at least knew that much—but he made a mental note to check the oil the next time he stopped for gas. And to test the tension of the fan belt to see if it was tight enough. Because if it isn't, the generator runs down. Or something.

He looked up to see that a young woman holding a small child was standing near him looking under the hood. She asked if he was having trouble and he said that he wasn't. And laughed.

That was how this wonderful day had got started!

She was about twenty-four, short, chubby, with long blond

hair. Wore glasses. Had a nice smile. The boy she was holding was about a year old. He, too, was chubby and blond, like his mother. And had a cute smile.

Apparently he was learning how to wave to people, and he practiced on Toomey, who waved back. And the mother looked at the boy and smiled and was pleased that he and this nice man were smiling and waving at each other.

Toomey smiled broadly. He always got a nice feeling from this kind of thing. He said, "Good-looking little boy you got."

She said, "Thank you."

"What's his name?"

When she said, "John," Toomey laughed. And because the mother didn't understand why he was laughing, he explained.

"That used to be my name."

She still didn't understand, probably, but she said, "Oh!" and laughed, too, And Toomey slammed down the hood.

He got into the car and closed the door.

The mother was still standing there, waiting for someone, probably. Her husband, likely. And she called to him. "Have a good day."

He said, "You, too." And while he backed up he waved some more to the boy and the boy waved back.

That was good. He liked that. And he hoped they were happy.

Then he looked back to make sure he wasn't about to bump into someone.

About that time a black-handled screwdriver rolled off the fender and under the white four-door Dodge that had been parked next to his car.

Before he left the parking lot, Toomey remembered something and almost turned back. What he had remembered was that earlier he had thought it would be a good idea if he bought a gift of some kind and left it in her car. Something from the inn gift shop. A card, maybe. Or a box of candy.

He felt bad about forgetting. But he didn't turn back.

He passed through a large shopping center. He could have

stopped and had a cup of coffee at the drugstore, but that would not have been truly in accordance with the spirit of the agreement. And he wanted to be able to tell her honestly that he had done what he had said he would do. Had gone for a drive and had found a place where it was peaceful and quiet and where a person could do some serious thinking.

A couple of miles past the shopping center he turned left onto a dirt road. He drove on that road for another couple of miles. There was a small brook running parallel to the road, now, and summer cottages, occasionally, all empty and boarded up. And silence. Large quantities of it. Just ahead was a small bridge and just short of that Toomey pulled off the road and stopped the motor. And got out.

There was no sound except the whisper of the water as it moved across and around the rocks. No bird calls, of course. This was December. Not even a squirrel scurrying. Or leaf falling.

The only sounds here were the sounds he himself made. And when the door closed behind him he almost felt like apologizing for the loud noise.

It would not be completely accurate to say that he held a serious discussion with himself as to whether or not he should return to the inn. Or simply continue on his way. He had made up his mind even before he left the parking lot. But he went through the formalities.

He told himself that there is more to life than just having a woman. Or, if you do want a woman, is it necessary to take the relationship as seriously as he seemed always to take it? It is possible that she was right when she said that he was simply overromantic and would fall in love permanently with the first woman who smiled nicely at him.

It had been a good day. He had twice made love to a beautiful woman. Most pleasurably.

Maybe he should continue on his way, and tomorrow find another woman and make love to her. And enjoy. And continue on his way.

The world is full of women, you know.

And there is more to life than just loving a woman.

He studied the things around him, felt the wooden railings of the bridge and the moss on the rocks and thought a moment on the many forms of life growing all about him. Saw things that had been cut down in their prime. Saw rotting stumps and tiny saplings and stones and leaves and a nest, open against the sky now that the leaves had fallen to the ground. And watched a small white cloud breaking up as it made its way across the sky. Until there was no sign of it. Nothing to show that only a few minutes ago it had been there. Up there. There, somewhere.

That was it, and it was good. He was satisfied with it. Glad to be part of it. Even though you disappear in the end. There was much to delight in, still.

Like being in love. Which brought him back full circle.

And he suddenly felt the strong need to get back to her and tell her about it.

He would start by telling her how he had carried out his part of the agreement. Where he had gone. The peace and the silence.

He would say, I walked where it was quiet and there was nothing to disturb my thoughts or influence my thinking in any way. And I asked myself if I wanted to be with you forever. And decided that I did.

I looked to see if there was anything there as beautiful as your face. And there wasn't. I felt things to see if anything was as soft and firm as you. Fragrant as your breath, earthshaking as your smile. Or even anything there at all that wouldn't be improved by my sharing it with you.

There was, by the side of the road, an old and empty mayonnaise jar. And Toomey took it to the brook and with some sand washed the label off. There were no flowers to be found, of course, but there were green ferns by the edge of the brook. And in the brook he found small pebbles, some with color to them, filled the jar with the pebbles and water and ferns. And a few small brown dried skeletons of flowers or weeds. No difference. They looked nice.

Not exactly a vase of beautiful flowers, but he was happy with it.

She would like it. And it would be his proof that he had gone to the countryside, as he had promised, to think it over.

By this time it was almost dark and Toomey realized that he had stayed here longer than he should have.

He hurried back to the car and got in and turned the key in the ignition.

16

Toni ordered a cup of coffee, then changed her mind.

"I'll have another beer."

But when the waitress came back with it, Toni again had changed her mind.

She still wanted the beer, but sitting here drinking it by herself was dumb. George should be here drinking it with her. And he probably had not yet left the parking lot.

"I still want the beer," she said, "but I want to go to the parking lot for a moment. But I'll be right back."

And she started to get up.

The waitress didn't look too happy about that. The man had gone and now the woman, too, wanted to go. And the check still had not been paid.

Toni saw the look of concern on the woman's face.

"I'll pay the bill first," she said, "if that will make you feel better."

She took money from her purse, and waited while the waitress figured out how much was owed. Plus tax. And because the waitress apparently was new to the job, it took a while.

By the time she got outside, another car was pulling into the space that George had vacated. She saw his car—or one that looked like his—at that moment pulling onto the highway and heading east. And she swore under her breath and watched it until it passed out of sight.

She did not intend to get into her own car and make that same kind of unnecessary trip out and back.

She looked over at her car and the thought came to her that she didn't care if she ever got back into it.

Maybe tonight she and George would meet some nice young couple, broke, down on their luck, maybe hitchhiking, and she'd give them her car and say that she didn't need it anymore. And she'd get into George's car and they'd swing by her house and pick up Myra and then they'd go away someplace for a long time.

She was tired of cars. Tired of being a mechanic. Tired of new cars, old cars, broken-down cars. She was tired of the garage, the dirt, the grease, the dumb customers. The noise, lunch from a paper bag, and the sameness of one day following the next.

It would be nice to have her mornings free to take Myra to the park or playground or museum, and put her down, herself, for her afternoon nap. Rather than some teacher's aide at the day-care center. And when Myra went to school, Toni wanted to be there when she got home.

And she wanted to be able to take her car to the garage for its regular checkup and tell the man that she'd be back to pick it up about four.

My husband will drop me off.

And be sure to test the sparkplugs and points. The car's been running a bit rough lately.

When she went back up to the room, she found, of course,

that his bag was gone. As expected. Still, the absence of it sent a small worrisome stab through her.

He would return, though, she knew, sure as her name was Maggie O'Reilly.

She took off her dress—it had done its job—kicked off her shoes, and from the suitcase took a pair of loafers, a pair of dungarees, and a sweater. But before she put them on, she sat for a moment on the edge of the bed, remembering.

She remembered his shyness, the long time it had taken him to get into bed, how cautiously he had first touched her, and how she'd had to pull him over and into her.

She recalled the feel of him, the bulk of him. His big hands alongside her face and his trying to explain about the pulsations and the waves of tenderness.

And she laughed as she remembered how he had collapsed with such shaking and breaking. And how he had said thank you, Maggie, and she had said thank you!

She lay down on the bed, on her back, and let the feelings of all of it come over her once more. She felt it all happening again. She touched the places he had touched and rubbed the parts where he had rubbed and recalled the smell of him, the bulk of him.

It was almost as if he were there again with her and she cried out softly at the pleasure of it. And ran her hand along the pillow where his head had lain.

Later, she rubbed both hands happily across her stomach.

She was at that moment in the process of becoming pregnant. She felt sure of that.

The time spent waiting for five o'clock came fast enough. And entertainingly.

She flew milkweed seeds and talked to a writer about a story he was working on.

The milkweed seeds she found while walking in the field beyond the mown part of the inn property. A dozen or more of the large brown pods were only partly open, so she broke the shells the rest of the way and filled the breeze with small parachutes. Tiny black seeds trailing long white threads.

Once, not caring how it might look to anyone looking out the windows of the inn, she ran alongside them a little way, catching some and releasing them again.

That was fun.

The writer she found sitting on a lawn chair on the terrace. A small, balding, middle-aged man with a gray beard. He had been watching her. There was a chair next to him and because he spoke to her, she sat with him for a while.

He told her it had been delightful to see her running in the field, and she said thank you.

She said that she had been helping some milkweed seeds get on about their business, and he said that that had been good of her.

He told her his name, and she told him part of hers. Her new one.

"Maggie."

He seemed to like that.

"I'm half Irish."

"Oh, really?"

That was what he was supposed to say, but she got laughing so hard that she couldn't deliver the punch line properly and when she did get it out it didn't seem funny at all.

After they had talked a while about the inn and other things, he said that he was a writer and was spending the night here because he was writing a novel that had a place like this in it.

He didn't want to talk about the story, except to say that it was a romance. When she asked if it had a happy ending he said no.

Later he asked her if she would have dinner with him and was disappointed when she said that she couldn't.

By now the sun had almost set, a chill breeze was coming across the fields, and it was suddenly cold. Her friend said that he thought it was going to rain and she agreed.

She felt tired, for some reason. And the thought of a dinner, drink, and bed pleased her.

She said that she had to be going, then went into the bar to wait for George. Unless, of course, he was already there.

He wasn't. Which was good. It would be fun to see the look on his face as he came through the door.

He would be surprised to see her, of course. He'd say that he couldn't believe it was true, her being there.

The only reason I stayed, she'd say, is that I don't have the heart to see someone as dumb and innocent as you walk around unprotected.

You wouldn't make it as far as Boston.

She'd say, You'd pledge your eternal loyalty to the first waitress who managed to pour your coffee without spilling most of it in your lap.

(He'd say, What's wrong with spilling coffee in a man's lap?)

The first woman who smiles nicely and looks as if she needs someone to care for her will tie you into a lifetime contract and you'll spend the rest of your life doing nice things for her because it makes her smile. And get nothing in return except trouble.

She waited until a quarter after six. An hour and fifteen minutes past the time that he had said that he would be back, if he was going to be back at all.

Twice she had got up and gone into the dining room to see if by chance there had been a misunderstanding and he had thought it was there they had agreed to meet. But he wasn't there.

She took a few more minutes to finish her drink, and then at six-thirty smiled one last time at the nice bartender, left a good tip, got into her car, and headed home.

She could hardly believe it. And she stopped at the first restaurant she came to on the turnpike to think about it. And to kick herself a few times for being such a fool.

The first man she had met for years that she could love, and when he tells her that he has fallen in love with her, she says that she isn't interested.

And somewhere at about this time, somewhere between

153

here and the cape, the poor dumb son of a bitch was probably walking into a bar or restaurant where some waitress would ask him why he was looking so sad and he'd tell her and she would say, well, you come home with me tonight and I'll make you forget that foolish woman you met today.

God damn!

She tried to pull herself together. This was crazy. For one thing, she knew almost nothing about the man. He might have turned out to be a smashing bore, once she'd got to know him. Maybe he had some dumb hobby that she'd find intolerable. Or feelings about religion or art or politics that she couldn't abide. Maybe he snored or told stupid jokes.

He was headed for trouble. That was certain. You can't just tell someone who smiles at you that you love her. That's asking to be hurt. And she was glad that she wouldn't have to be around to see it.

She only hoped that he wouldn't be hurt too much.

Anyway—and she crushed out her cigarette—it had been fun for a day. He'd had a good sense of humor. And they'd had some laughs. And he was intelligent. She liked that. But, and she laughed to herself, he sure didn't know much about automobiles.

She wondered if he'd even be able to get his car started.

And suddenly felt sick at her stomach.

What if he'd not got back on time because he hadn't been able to get his car started! She'd never forgive herself.

Toni threw some money down and hurried for the door.

The bartender told her that the big man she'd described had shown up about twenty minutes after she'd gone. And he had asked if a woman, who fit Toni's description, had been there waiting.

"Did you tell him that I waited until six-thirty?"

He said that he had.

"I even took the liberty of telling him that you had seemed unhappy that he hadn't shown up."

He said, "I hope that was all right."

She said, "Sure. That was all right."

Then she asked, "He didn't leave a message or anything, did he?"

The bartender, a tall man about fifty years old, bald, looked as if he felt very bad about what had happened, as if it was part of his responsibility to see that things didn't go wrong while he was on duty.

"I guess I should have asked," he said. "But I didn't."

"What exactly, if anything, did he say?"

The bartender thought a moment.

"He had one shot of whiskey," he said. "Straight. Then left a dollar tip. And made some joke about how he had to go buy a sledgehammer and work on his car."

She said thanks, and left.

She hadn't cried since she was nine years old and she didn't want to do it now. At least not in front of anyone.

At the desk the clerk said that Mr. Daniels of room 342 had checked out half an hour ago.

"Are you sure?"

The clerk shrugged his shoulders. "That's what he said. He threw me the keys and said he was checking out.

"That's all I know."

During the drive home she reviewed all their conversations, searching for fragments that she might piece together for a clue that might lead to who he was or where he was from. But there was nothing. He had mentioned working at a place where there were sick people. And there had been mention of college and football. And he had come from a small town in Indiana. His car had had Connecticut license plates.

But she didn't know his name. And you can't find someone if you don't know his name.

At ten o'clock that night, about the time Toni Heller was pulling into her driveway in Coultraine, Toomey Bougereau was finishing a cup of coffee in a roadside restaurant west of Worcester. The waitress came over and asked if everything was all right. And he said that it was.

He had a road map spread open in front of him.

155

"Could I help you find what you're looking for?"

He shook his head.

"You look like you've had a hard trip," she said, and gave him a nice smile. "I'll get you another cup of coffee. On the house."

He said, "No thanks." And didn't bother to look up.

It was right there on the map. Munsen.

And just north of it was a town called Farmington. Where she and her friend had desegregated the men's sauna in the Farmington Hotel.

He folded the map, left the waitress fifty cents, got back on the turnpike and headed west.

In Munsen he ran into a man named Harvey. He rented a building from him and went into business. Spent a lot of time looking at people and attended everything, like basketball games or public meetings, where a big crowd would turn out.

Friday night, which was the big shopping night in Farmington, and Saturday afternoons, you could have found him somewhere on Main Street, probably near the Farmington Bank and Trust Company, looking at the faces of the women passing by.

If he had stayed in the area long enough, he might have become a legendary figure.

The old man, gray, bearded, who, people say, has stood in front of the Farmington Bank and Trust Company every Friday night and Saturday afternoon for many years, rain or shine, snow sometimes, looking intently into the faces of the female passersby.

What stories would have been invented as to why he was there! And he might have become a kind of tourist attraction, even. In the winter time, snow settling upon his bare head, still there, intense eyes always searching.

But he wasn't around for more than ten months. And you can't properly develop a legendary figure in that short a period of time.

17

Mrs. Murphey came into the office to say that Yolanda was quitting.

"How come?"

"She's going back to college in the fall so she wants to take August off."

"That's too bad," Toomey said. "I liked her. Roman did, too."

"She was a good worker."

"You've already found someone to replace her, I suppose."

She had. Subject to his approval, of course.

"It's all right with me," Toomey said. "From now on I want you to do the hiring. Your record is better than mine."

She nodded. You could tell that she agreed with that. He *did* seem to hire the kind of person who anyone with any perspicacity whatsoever could tell would end up causing trouble.

"Who do you have to replace her?"

"A college friend of hers. Yolanda brought her in yesterday

while you were out. A girl named Rosa. She, too, is going back to school in the fall, but she can work four weeks. And she said she needed the money."

"Sounds good."

"She's very intelligent," Mrs. Murphey said.

"Good."

"She's a psychology student. Yolanda said that she's into astral travel and extrasensory perception."

"Good," Toomey said. "We haven't had that yet."

Mrs. Murphey had something else to mention.

"My daughter, Myra's mother, is planning to come and spend all next week with me. For her vacation. So you'll finally get to meet her."

Toomey said that he was glad to hear that. "She must be a very nice person."

"She is. She's very attractive. And got a good head on her shoulders, too."

That sounded ideal. Toomey said that he'd be looking forward to it. "I'll even take her fishing, if she'd like to go."

"I'm sure she would."

That was nice. They smiled at each other. Then she went back into the shop and he answered the phone.

It was Lorraine. She wanted to know if Toomey would do something for her. A special favor.

He asked what.

She said she wanted him to make another big basket of the kind he'd made for her a few months ago. Lorraine's friend, Kate, had admired the one Lorraine had.

Could Toomey make it for her by tonight?

"I can't tonight," Toomey said. "I'm going fishing after work."

"How long would it take you?"

"An hour. At least."

She said please, and made kissing sounds over the phone and told him how sweet he was and how she wanted it by tonight because today was Kate's birthday. She wanted to give the basket to Kate as a birthday present.

Toomey finally said okay. He'd do it.

She said, "You're a doll."

"I'm not a doll," he said. "I'm doing it only because it's her birthday and I'm sentimental about birthdays. If it's her birthday and she wants a big basket, then she should have one."

"I'm taking her out to dinner," Lorraine said. "Then I want to give it to her as a surprise after we come back to my place."

She said, "Could you have it there by nine?"

"You told me she was married," Toomey said. "So how come her husband isn't taking her out to dinner?"

She said because Kate would rather go out to dinner with her and for Toomey not to worry his nice handsome head about such matters. And Toomey said that something about the whole deal made him feel a little uncomfortable and that he didn't like it.

Finally, he said, "I'll make it on one condition."

"What's that?"

"That you make it clear to her that you bought it from me. As a present from you to her. And not that it is something I made for her."

"That's what I'd planned to do."

"Good. I don't believe in a husband hearing that a man is giving something to his wife. Even if it's something she wants very much."

She said, "You're such a Puritan." And made more kissing noises over the phone and told him again how sweet he was and said she was counting on him and would expect him about nine.

Toomey worked a while in the shop, told Yolanda how sorry he was that she was leaving, and turned down for the twentieth time the suggestion that the workers be allowed to smoke grass while they worked.

Nick Nicocci called.

Nick said that he'd got a call from a Reverend Osterman in Farmington. And what was this about one of the girls being missing? And probably a suicide.

Toomey said that the girl had probably taken off for a while, as she was in the habit of doing. He said he had the feeling that she had hitchhiked to New Jersey, probably getting a ride from a middle-aged salesman. He remembered her saying once that she had a friend in Wyckoff, New Jersey.

"I expect to hear from her about the first of next week."

"The reverend insisted I come around and talk with you about it," Nick told him.

Toomey said, "Any time."

Nick changed the subject. "How's the fishing?"

Toomey said that the fishing was good but that his luck had been bad. He told how he had hooked a really big one two nights ago over by the lily pads, but it had got away. A really big one. Jumped out of the water once and came down with such a splash that it made waves that rocked the boat.

"That's hell," Nick said. "When the big ones get away. Ruins your whole day."

"That's true." Toomey said, "I had one get away last December, through my own fault, and I'm still kicking myself. I think it ruined not only my whole day, but maybe my whole life."

"What you got to do," Nick said, "is, after you first hook them, get them as soon as possible away from the lily pads and out into the open water."

Toomey said that that was what he had tried to do.

"Anyway, I got to come around and see you, so I can call the reverend back and tell him I did so."

"Always glad to see you," Toomey said.

"And one of these nights I'm going to come by your place after work and I'll show you how to get the big ones and not let them get away."

Toomey suggested he make it some time soon, because he'd been thinking about getting away for a little vacation.

Toomey went back to his pile of unpaid bills once more, trying to arrive at an estimate regarding the balance between debits and credits. But the only conclusion he reached was that it's hard to concentrate on bills when the weather is hot.

He diverted himself by lighting up another cigar and pouring a tiny bit of bourbon into a paper cup. So little that a fly landing in it would not have done more than get its feet wet. But it was better than none at all and he pushed the pile of bills off to one side, leaned back, and relaxed, and let his thoughts go back to the conversation with Nick. Not about Angela. He wasn't worried about her. But about that big fish he had almost caught the other night.

He looked out the window toward the lake.

In order to get that big, that fish must have been pretty smart. Because when you hang around those particular lily pads during fishing season, one mistake could be fatal.

Unless, of course, you make that mistake when you are very young. In which case you're caught and then thrown back.

He thought about that for a moment, and decided it was worth passing along to Myra and Roman.

Myra was on the floor, cutting out pictures from the Sunday *Boston Globe;* Roman was taking a late afternoon nap.

"Kids, the time to make mistakes is when you're young."

He took a small sip, just enough to wet his lips. And thought about it some more.

Probably about now that fish's mouth has stopped hurting and he or she has stopped berating himself or herself for being so dumb at such an advanced age.

That was something Toomey could relate to. You get old enough to think that you're grown up and you find yourself still doing dumb things. And chances are that the next thing you do will be as dumb as the thing you kicked yourself for doing only a week ago. So you have to do a lot of things wrong. And that takes a lot of time.

That thought, too, he summarized and passed along to his friends. In case they were worried about doing dumb things.

He said, "It takes a long time to grow up."

One last sip, then he tossed the paper cup into the wastebasket.

"In years to come," he said, "you can tell people that you and Toomey Bougereau grew up together."

Roman thumped his tail three times.

Myra made a final cut with her scissors, then held up the figure of a dog cut from one of the pictures. And Toomey nodded approvingly. Good work.

Then he said, quickly, "Ketchup."

She said, "Hamburger." Then she said, "Damn." And hit her hand on the floor.

Toomey reached out and made a mark beneath his name on the wall.

"That's the third time I got you with that one."

But he shook his head. "You're still way ahead of me, though. Twenty-eight to nine."

She casually turned a page or two of the newspaper, looking for something that needed cutting out.

"Ice cream."

He said, "Pencils."

Toomey was a little late getting to Lorraine's house that night and when he finally did arrive he found that she and her friend, Kate, were already a number of drinks ahead of him. Both had got into something more comfortable, had taken their shoes off, and were sitting on the sofa with their legs tucked under them.

They were discussing what had recently become an increasingly popular subject of conversation between them. Namely, how awful men are, how women are abused everywhere, and why women must now stand up for their rights.

He walked in just as Kate was finishing a story about something someone had said at last night's meeting of the Munsen Women's Organization.

"And when she finished," and Kate made a big upward sweeping motion like an orchestra conductor signaling for a mighty increase in volume, "as with one voice, everyone in the room shouted, *'Then leave him!'* "

It might well have been one of the big dramatic moments of recent years.

And there was Toomey, feeling silly as hell, just standing there holding a big wicker basket.

To Kate, Lorraine said, "That's so wonderful!" Referring to the dramatic ending.

And to Toomey, as she got off the couch, "You silly!" And

gave him a look of dramatic reproach.

"I didn't want you to just come *in* with it. I wanted it to be a *surprise*."

She turned to Kate. "Darling, this was to be a surprise for you. For your birthday. It's just like the one that I have. The one that you like so much."

Kate was delighted. Overwhelmed, almost. She got to her feet, embraced Lorraine, and said, "Thank you so very much."

It was a very moving scene and Toomey moved over and fixed himself a drink.

After they had pulled apart, Lorraine said, "Tell Toomey that other thing that someone said that I thought was funny."

Kate either didn't remember it or didn't want to repeat it. So Lorraine told it.

"It was about the woman who had seen the TV advertisement about the toilet tissue that was soft and absorbent, but strong. And she said that that was what every husband wanted his wife to be like. Soft and absorbent, but strong. Like toilet paper."

Toomey had started toward a chair, but turned around and went back to the liquor cabinet and added a little more whiskey.

Kate said, "I was only repeating what someone said. I didn't mean to imply that everyone thought it was funny. Or profound."

Lorraine said that she was really in agreement with Kate and that it had not been funny. What she meant was that it had been clever of the woman to recognize that similarity.

Before Toomey got back to his chair, Lorraine asked if he would fix them both another drink, and held out her glass.

Things were quiet for a few moments and Toomey was aware that his presence was detracting from the party spirit that had prevailed before he got there. And he began making up a plausible reason for having to get home early.

He and Kate had never particularly enjoyed each other's company, anyway. She was nice enough, and attractive, but had an expression on her face that implied that she knew you were planning to say something insulting, and that you had better not.

She had two young children and a husband who spent most evenings with his friends from the paper mill, where he worked, drinking beer and playing pool at the Veterans of Foreign Wars clubhouse in Munsen.

If they were trying to celebrate Kate's birthday by getting drunk, they were succeeding. Which had a sobering effect on Toomey.

After a while, Lorraine got very affectionate. She came up to Toomey, kissed him, spilling a little of her drink on him as she did so, reached down and rubbed her hands along his thighs and in between. And said things like how great a lover he was and how much she enjoyed being in bed with him. But she wasn't talking to him as much as she was describing him for Kate's benefit. And she motioned for Kate to come closer.

So Kate came over and spilled a little of her drink on him, too. And for a few moments the three of them stood there, a small group weaving disjointedly back and forth, Toomey trying to ward off their drinks and at the same time managing to keep them on their feet.

They circled around slowly, holding one another, trying to keep upright. With Toomey feeling more sober all the time and wondering what the hell had happened to whiskey these days that it didn't have the strength it used to.

Lorraine said, "I want to make love to you, you big lovable old bear!" And she pushed herself up against Toomey and put two arms and one drink around his neck.

"And I want Kate to come with us."

Toomey managed to get his drink down on the table before Kate edged in even closer to show that she was ready for anything.

He got their drinks away from them. One at a time. And got them upstairs and into Lorraine's bedroom. There he did a little rubbing himself. Spreading his broad hands across their breasts and rear ends and everywhere else he thought they'd enjoy it.

"You two get your clothes off and into bed," Toomey said, "and I'll fix you both another drink. And be under the covers when I get back."

They told him to hurry up, and he said that he would. He got them to sit on the edge of the bed, and by the time he left the room they were helping each other unfasten their zippers.

They were in bed, when he got back, naked, faces flushed, looking happy and expectant. They both raised up on their elbows when he came in, the covers falling down enough to show what sensual delights were waiting there for him to enjoy. And he handed them their drinks.

He reached down and patted all four soft warm white breasts, one at a time. Impartially. From right to left.

"I didn't fix one."

He remained standing. Looking down at them, smiling. At Lorraine, mostly.

This seemed like a nice way to end an affair that had pretty much run its course.

Lorraine said, "Aren't you going to take your clothes off and come to bed?"

He gave each of them one soft pat on the cheek, and shook his head.

He said, gently, "You two don't need me." And he gave them both a final, affectionate smile and turned toward the door.

As he left the room, Lorraine screamed after him, "God damn you, Toomey!

"Get out and stay out!"

18

Washing the dinner dishes is not in itself something that a person would choose as the most exciting way to spend one's life. But if you have a four-year-old daughter trying to help, that makes the chore at least challenging. It does not shorten the time required to do the job, of course. The opposite most certainly is true. But it does require some strategy and does provide the opportunity for developing quicker reflexes and proper timing.

Toni managed to slip a saucer past her daughter and onto the drying rack.

Myra, standing on a stool by the edge of the counter, contrived to intercept every third or fourth article that passed in front of her and work on it a bit with a dish towel. Or drop it. Or both.

Myra said, "If that pile of dishes gets any higher it will fall over and land on my head."

Toni slipped another saucer through, gave Myra a small

pan to dry, then got three plates across in quick succession.

"It's all right," Toni said. "Even if it did fall over I don't think it would land on your head."

She added a little more hot water and glanced up at the clock.

"You're supposed to say that maybe it will fall over and land on your nose."

Toni glanced again at the clock. Someone was coming by for her in an hour.

"It isn't going to fall over," Toni said. "And even if it did, it wouldn't land on my nose. My foot, maybe. But not my nose."

"Then say that. That it will land on your foot."

All right. Anything. Whatever amuses a four-year-old girl was all right with her.

"Maybe it will fall over," Toni said, "and land on my foot."

Myra laughed. So Toni laughed, too. Why not?

"If that pile of dishes gets any bigger," Myra said, "it will fall over and land on my ear." And she laughed with delight.

Hearing your daughter laugh with delight is delightful indeed. So Toni laughed with delight, too. And slipped two cups quickly past her young helper.

She tried chin next, and that got a good response. Myra used big toe, which was pretty funny, and got long laughs from both of them. And then they used up more and more parts of the anatomy until Myra topped it off with, "If that pile of dishes gets any bigger it will fall over and land on my *belly button!*"

And that brought the three women down from upstairs to find out what all the laughing was about.

"Where did you learn that funny game?"

Myra said that she and Toomey played it a lot.

"I should have guessed."

"He's funny," Myra said. "Like Uncle Mike."

Toni said, "That's nice."

Her Uncle Mike was the only person to whom Toni had told the full story of what had happened that first Thursday of December along the Massachusetts Turnpike and later at the Merritt Inn.

168

She had told him about it one night in his kitchen, drinking beer and listening—half listening—to the Red Sox baseball game on the radio. They were playing the Yankees and it probably was an important game.

"You would have liked him," she said. "He had a good sense of humor. And a good laugh. Kind of deep and easy."

Mike nodded. Up to this point of the story he had not said much. Only listened.

On the radio someone had got a hit and someone else had moved from first to third.

That had been a Friday night. Myra was in Munsen with her grandmother and Aunt Evelyn was out on some kind of church business. Mike had not known what kind of business it was specifically. The church was now the major part of her life and he didn't try to keep track of all the parts of it that she was into, which committees she was on, what it was she was attending or managing. He had stopped going to church years ago. Even if they passed a rule permitting smoking during services, he probably still wouldn't go.

Mike was one of three brothers. All of them, like Toni's father, had been strong union men. Politically, he was off to the left somewhere. In the sixties he had worked for civil rights and had marched in peace parades and taken part in demonstrations and other forms of protest against the Vietnam war.

He and Evelyn had two sons. Both were in Canada. One had gone there in 1967 because he refused to be drafted for the war, and the younger brother had joined him a year later. For the same reason. Both were married, now, working, and neither intended to return to the States. But they were bitter, seldom wrote, and Mike was left with the feeling that he had failed them. And himself.

It was not an easy feeling to live with.

He didn't talk about it much.

Once, sitting at the table as they now were, Toni had said that it was too bad he and Aunt Evelyn hadn't had a girl.

Mike was skeptical. He said. "She'd probably have been a nun."

The fans at Fenway Park were yelling about something and

after a moment the announcer came on to tell about someone hitting a double and two runs scoring.

Good for someone. Good for all three of them, in fact.

"Do you know who's winning?"

He said, "Boston."

She said, "I keep going back over the things he said he did as part of his work. He said, for instance, that he dealt with people. I remember that because I made a joke about him being a professional cardplayer."

Mike liked that.

"What did he say he did?"

"He didn't say specifically what it was, of course, because I'd asked him not to. But he said that in his job he had to have a lot of patience, keep his mouth shut, be encouraging, and not get bored at hearing the same old excuses over and over again."

Mike said, "The man runs a garage."

And they both laughed a little.

Not very much.

"I was joking," Mike said. "If I were to guess, I'd say he was a schoolteacher. Except for that part about keeping your mouth shut."

He got up and got another beer from the refrigerator. And while he was up, another cigar.

She asked him when he was going to go see a doctor.

"Don't change the subject. I'm trying to think of what it is your friend does for a living. If we knew what he does for a living, we might be able to locate him."

She said, "If I were Aunt Evelyn, I'd make you go."

He had lost a lot of weight in the last six months. And was tired a lot. He said it was because he'd cut down on his pastrami sandwiches.

Besides, he liked being thin.

Mike sat back down.

He said, "Maybe it's possible he was a priest or minister. Did you notice anything peculiar about his collar?"

She said, "It was kind of wrinkled. I think probably he does his own laundry."

"Then he wasn't a priest."

He asked again, "You sure you don't want another beer?"

"Okay, I guess I do."

He started to get up, but she said, "I'll get it."

Someone struck out and the inning was over and some automobile manufacturer took that opportunity to say some good things about his product.

"Come to think of it," Toni said. "He might have been a doctor."

After a moment, Mike said, "That's a good straight line. But I can't follow it with any remark of the kind I think an uncle should say to his niece."

She said, "Something I remember is interesting."

"Like what?"

"We were talking about different kinds of diseases. Diabetes, Parkinson's disease, heart trouble. And later when he was referring to the same kind of thing, he used the expression cardiac arrest. I remember that because I made some joke about not ever having been arrested for anything."

"Sounds like you two had some fascinating conversations. Who had which diseases. And how often."

"They were fun," she said. And drank some of her beer.

"Did you tell him you were an automobile mechanic?"

She shook her head.

Someone grounded out to someone.

"If he wasn't a priest or a teacher," Mike said, "then he must have been a psychoanalyst. Or a counselor of some kind. They sit and listen to people's troubles."

She said that she had thought of that. "He might have been a counselor of some kind."

"Counselors have to have patience and not talk too much," Mike said. "And they have to listen to the same problems and excuses over and over again."

"Something like that, probably."

Mike said, "Maybe he was a sex therapist. Or a marriage counselor."

"I don't think he was a sex therapist," Toni said. "And he'd been married twice. And divorced twice."

"Then he was probably a marriage counselor."

Toni said, "When are you going to make an appointment with the doctor?"

Mike said, "One of these days." And asked, "Did he try to talk you into getting married?"

"He didn't say anything about that."

"Then he's a marriage counselor."

He re-lit the cigar and nodded his head. That was his final opinion on the matter.

"You had a brief affair with a marriage counselor."

Later he asked if his joking about the matter was inappropriate.

She said, "Of course not. What do you think I'm supposed to do? Sit around and cry about it?"

"Of course not. You're too big a person for that."

"I should think so."

And she felt pretty close to crying right at that moment.

"You know, of course, that any time things get rough there's always room for you and Myra here. And any others you decide to have. If you end up with six children we'll add a couple bedrooms."

"Thanks."

Apparently someone hit a home run. The announcer was so excited he was practically incoherent.

"What happened?"

Mike said, "I don't know. But if the Sox don't win this game they're in trouble."

The noise subsided and the announcer gave the unhappy news that Roy White of the New York Yankees had just hit his fourteenth homer of the year, this time with the bases loaded. Making the score seven to three.

"So they're in trouble."

Toni said, "That's too bad."

The situation at the house was not as good as it had once been. Maxine had had an affair with an older man and it had not ended well. She had not especially cared for him and wouldn't have married him anyway, but he had made certain promises that he hadn't kept. Maxine didn't have a summer job and didn't want to have to go back to her parents, so she was down on men and life in general. And the other two women hadn't had anything good to say about the masculine side of the human race for a number of months. Consequently, the viewpoints expressed around the house were at times in conflict with the thoughts running through Toni's mind. It is not easy to be sympathetic to the point of view that women are better off without men when you are straining your brain trying to think of a way to locate a certain one of them.

They knew most of the story by now, but not the details. Maxine had told them what Toni planned to do, and when she returned that night in December they had assumed that everything had happened as planned. And they would have continued to believe that, had not some friends been visiting one night and Maxine had started praising Toni as one of the most liberated women you would ever expect to see. Who liked and wanted children but didn't need men. Who was self-supporting and independent. Who didn't know the name or whereabouts of the father of the child she was carrying, and didn't want to know.

Toni admitted that it wasn't quite that way. She wished that she did know both his name and his whereabouts. So she could go looking for him.

"I thought you didn't want to know his name. Or to let him know yours, either."

That, unfortunately, was what she had succeeded in doing. But the problem was that she had fallen in love with him. And now she wanted him.

One of the guests said that she thought that in our society we tend to overemphasize the need for men.

Toni could agree with that, in part. One could get along without them, she supposed.

"But this particular one would be very nice to have around. To go swimming with, to bed with, or just sit across the table from and talk and drink beer with."

So at the house they now looked at her a little differently. She was only another example of how it is that when a man and a woman have a love affair, if one of them gets pregnant it is always the woman.

One night, again drinking beer with her Uncle Mike in the kitchen and half-listening to the ball game, she told him that it amused her that her mother was trying to fix her up with her boss. The man named Toomey.

"Why don't you let her?"

She didn't say anything right away, so Mike said, "You don't really expect to run into that man again, do you?"

She nodded her head. "Someday."

Mike shook his head. He didn't think she would.

"That Toomey person might be worth taking a look at. If he wants to give up that basket business, maybe we can make a good mechanic out of him."

She was skeptical, but she did say that she'd at least meet him.

The next Saturday afternoon, when she was over visiting her mother in Munsen, Toni did take Myra for a walk downtown and over to the brown-shingled little house near Baskets and Baskets. She wanted to introduce herself to that Toomey person and thank him for letting Myra play in his office so much.

But he wasn't home.

She told Mike later that her mother said Toomey was away a lot on weekends. Spent much of the time up in Farmington.

"Probably got a woman there," Mike said.

"Probably."

The last time she sat with her uncle in the kitchen was the night after he had finally made an appointment with the doctor. He wouldn't talk about it, though, except to say that it was for the next day.

He asked, "How's Myra?"

"She's fine. I told Mother I'll be coming over Friday night and that I'll spend next week over there with her. And then I'll bring Myra back here."

"Good."

"She said to tell you hello."

"Thanks."

"She also said to tell you that she and Toomey Bougereau are growing up together."

They agreed that that was nice.

19

In his office one afternoon Toomey looked into his upside-down shot glass and asked if he would ever again see the beautiful woman who had called herself Maggie O'Reilly.

The answer came back no. He wouldn't. Never again.

He'd had his one chance and lost it.

He talked to Myra about it. She was the only one he knew who would understand.

She was sharpening pencils at the time and possibly couldn't even hear what he was saying. Which was just as well. One thing an adult shouldn't do is lay his troubles on a small child.

"Life isn't all winning," he said. "So one of the things you got to learn is to be able to lose."

That was such an obvious observation that she didn't even bother to turn her head.

He said, "Like sometimes you get a pencil sharpened to just

the perfect point and you set it on the table and it falls off and rolls behind the radiator."

Just at that moment she finished sharpening a pencil, but dropped it and broke the point. She picked it up, shook her head as if discouraged by her clumsiness, then put it back into the sharpener and went to work on it again. And after a few moments had it as good as it had been the first time.

"You're a good kid," Toomey said. "You'll make out all right."

Roman thumped his tail four times.

Despite the prediction that he would never see Maggie again, he didn't give up hope. Probably not even Madeline herself had been right 100 percent of the time. So Saturday afternoons he went up to Farmington and walked along Main Street looking closely at the faces of the women. And whenever there was a big concert or play or large gathering of any kind he always went and looked the crowd over very carefully.

Once a Woody Allen movie was playing and he felt sure that if she were in town she'd go see that. And he stood in front of the theatre the first three nights and watched everyone who went in or came out.

He wasted one night at the Farmington Hilton bar, which was obviously not the kind of place she'd go to. Very plush, restrained, older people, mostly, with coats and ties and no laughter.

He saw no one who looked like her, even at first glance. And no one he would have wanted instead of her.

Then one day as he was leaving his office he got the idea that he should have thought of long ago.

Some high-school kids passing by the building were what made him think of it.

She had probably grown up in Munsen. So if he could get a look at the high-school yearbooks covering the years that she was in school, somewhere in the pages of the individual pictures of the graduating class, he'd see that face. A little different, of course. More youthful. But he'd recognize it right away. He knew that.

He went down to Harvey's the next morning and asked

Harvey where the kids in town went to high school. And was told that they went to Harmon County Regional High School just across the line in Hartsville. Kids from the town of Munsen, Hartsville, and West Hartsville went there.

He asked how to get there and Harvey gave him directions.

"Not that it is any of my business," Harvey said, "but why are you asking?"

Toomey said that he wanted to see if he could repeat his junior year.

"That was a good year. I wouldn't mind going through that one more time."

Some other people were in the store when he said that, and they thought that was funny and there was some joking about how those years were the best years of our lives. And Harvey contributed the observation that life gets hard after high school.

When Toomey got to the school he found that there weren't many people around, it being summer and no classes in session. But there were a few cars in the parking lot and the building was open.

He heard sounds coming from down a corridor and headed in that direction, coming finally to an office where a young girl about eighteen was typing behind a desk. A thin, petulant-looking short-haired blonde with a short typewriter eraser that she used twice before taking time to look up and ask Toomey what it was he wanted.

He could hear people talking in one of the rear rooms behind the partition.

Toomey said he was wondering if the school had copies of yearbooks from years past. And would she let him look at some.

She said, yes, they had copies. What years was he interested in looking at?

He had figured that Maggie was probably about thirty-one or thirty-two. And she had probably graduated at about age eighteen.

"About thirteen to fifteen years back, if you have them."

The girl said, "We don't have them more than eight years back."

And waited rather impatiently for his reaction to that.

"Are you sure?"

She nodded.

Toomey was not the kind of person who felt comfortable about asking someone to go to extra work, but this was important. So he asked, "Would you mind checking?"

She said, "I don't need to check. I know for sure." And she looked down at the typewriter and then back to him, meaning to show that she was really very busy.

"Do you know of any place where I could find yearbooks from that period?"

She said, "They're just not available, that's all. There just aren't any."

She turned back to her work, typed three more words, stomped her foot against the floor in irritation, and picked up the eraser once more.

Toomey said, "Thank you." And left.

The principal came out a moment later and asked what it was the man had wanted, and she told him.

"That's what I thought he was asking about," he said.

"Did you explain to him that the reason we have yearbooks going back only eight years is that Regional has been in existence only eight years?"

She said she hadn't.

He said, "That's too bad. He could get copies from the town where the student went to school before the Regional High School was established."

"Do you want me to go try to catch him before he gets away?"

The man said, "It's probably too late now."

Then he added, "But keep things like that in mind in the future."

Before going back into his office, he said, "I just hope it wasn't anything important. Government business or something."

On the way back to the shop Toomey found himself behind some people from Christian Bounty. You could tell that they were part of that organization because they had a bumper sticker on their car that said, HONK IF YOU LOVE JESUS.

Toomey honked, of course. He loved Jesus. Who doesn't? And the woman driving the car honked back and the people inside waved.

He waved back.

Toomey liked that. People honking and waving at one another in a friendly way is something this country could use more of.

He wondered if there was some kind of bumper sticker he could have printed to use for the back of his car.

HONK IF YOU LIKE BASKETS, maybe.

But he didn't like that. That wasn't good. It sounded more like a commercial message than an expression of friendliness.

Some people around town made fun of the Christian Bounty bumper stickers. People like Charlie Gibson, who pretended to get terribly excited at the sight of them. Honking and honking and waving and waving. It probably isn't true that he goes out of his way to look for them, although some people say that he does. But he never passes up the opportunity to honk and wave.

Charlie, himself, tells about the time that he and his cousin, Eddie, on their way to a softball game and beer party in Farmington, in separate cars, came upon a flock of Christian Bounty people at Park Circle. They both went wild, honking at every car, cutting in and out of traffic to make sure they didn't miss anyone, and all the Christian Bounty people honked back and waved and everybody went a second time around the circle just for the good sport of it.

One summer resident from New York City who saw it said that he hadn't heard anything like it since the time he was stuck in a taxi in midtown Manhattan late one afternoon when the traffic lights stopped working all along Fifth Avenue.

Two people from Christian Bounty came by to see Toomey that afternoon. They'd like to talk to him, they said, if he had a few minutes free.

He had the time, he said, but they'd have to talk to him in the shop because there was a girl napping on the couch in his office.

He persuaded the girls to turn the radio down enough so he

and the Christian Bounty people could hear one another if they shouted.

Of the two, the man was the older. About thirty. Thin, balding, black-framed glasses. The woman was in her early twenties. They were both good-looking, friendly, well mannered. They gave as their reason for coming the fact that they were interviewing all employers in the area regarding employment opportunities for their staff and students. Either part-time or full-time.

Toomey said he didn't anticipate needing to hire anyone for a while. That every time one of the girls was getting ready to leave, she told her friends and one of them was in asking for her job even before Toomey knew the girl was quitting.

They understood, and nodded. But if he didn't mind, could they just look around?

He didn't mind, of course. He even escorted them.

They kept a little ahead of him, talking to one another in low tones. Occasionally asking Toomey a question. Like what kind of heating did the building have and was it warm in the winter.

"Is this the only bathroom?"

Toomey said it was. The employees took turns using it.

Did the roof leak?

It didn't, Toomey said. Far as he'd noticed.

The man thought it unfortunate that the back wall didn't have any windows, and Toomey agreed. He said the lake was too far away, too, and they agreed with him on that.

All in all, it was a nice friendly visit. And when they left they said, "God bless you."

That was nice. Toomey said, "God bless you, too."

Mrs. Murphey said she thought they hadn't come to inquire about jobs, but only to look at the building.

They were probably planning to buy the place and make it into a dormitory. Or else, someone said, keep on making baskets but hire their own people.

While Myra was still napping, Toomey went down to Harvey's to buy some coloring books and to ask about Christian Bounty.

He asked if they were planning to buy the place.

"They'll buy anything they can get their hands on," Harvey said.

"What do they want to use it for?"

He didn't know the answer to that.

"Where do they get all their money?"

Harvey didn't know that, either. "But I know that they are going to have a big fund-raising gathering on their property next Sunday.

"Clambake, steak roast, the whole works. Someone said that they got people coming from all over New England and they expect to raise a quarter million dollars in pledges and donations."

"A quarter million dollars?"

"That's what I heard. And that is considered a conservative figure. It may go as high as a half million. Or more."

Toomey stood there for a moment. Silent. Head down a little.

Then he said, "Their fund-raising party is going to be a great disappointment, I fear."

He said, "You can quote me as predicting not only bad weather and a poor turnout, but donations and pledges that don't come to more than a fifth of what they expect."

Harvey shrugged his shoulders. And said, "You may be right."

"I'm sure I am."

"I'm not saying, myself. I don't have any crystal balls."

Toomey said, "Maybe you should stock them."

He said to add a dozen pencils to his order.

20

Mrs. Murphey was in the office first thing Monday morning to say that her daughter would not be spending the week here after all. She had to stay in Coultraine because of some problems at the garage. One of the other workers had been in an automobile accident and would be out for a week.

Toomey was disappointed. He also had an uneasy, disquieting feeling. As if maybe fate was getting a bit too much involved in Toomey's private affairs.

He had begun to visualize Myra's mother as a very nice person. Tall—since Myra was tall for her age—strong, independent, and with a good sense of humor. These being qualities he saw in Myra. And since there had never been any mention of Myra's father, he assumed that she was either widowed or divorced.

She might even have been someone who would have liked him, and someone he could have loved.

That would have been good.

"I am disappointed," Mrs. Murphey said.

Toomey said, "Me, too."

"You would have enjoyed meeting her."

"I'm sure I would have. Anyone who has a daughter as good as Myra must be a great person."

"She really is a great person," Mrs. Murphey said. "I've always been proud of her. I know you'd love her."

Okay, okay! Enough.

That's fate. Sometimes it brings nice things your way and sometimes it doesn't. And he changed the subject.

Later that morning Toomey stopped in at Harvey's to get some soda for the cooler and got the news about the big fund-raising outdoor party that Christian Bounty had held the day before. Under clear skies.

"I remember you predicted rain," Harvey said.

"Just a feeling I had."

"Well, they couldn't have had a better day for it. Bright sun, light breeze. And from what I heard this morning from an unofficial but reliable source, they raised a lot of money."

He said that he'd heard they had a lot of big money people there from all over New England.

Toomey said good for them.

"I understand that they raised even more money than they expected to."

"Well," Toomey said, "as you mentioned the other day, it's not easy to predict anything without a crystal ball."

He told Harvey he wanted to buy another Crazy Crawler. "I lost one the other night out on the lake."

It was noon by the time he got back to the office and the girls were out playing Frisbee during their lunch hour. A short distance from the building, Toomey stopped to chat with Bill Brinkman, local insurance agent and president of the Rotary Club, who had happened to run into Mort Feldman, Sr., who had a real estate office downtown. Probably Mort had been out getting some exercise and maybe Brinkman had followed him to this somewhat off the beaten path part of town to try to sell him some insurance.

Anyway, they were chatting in a friendly way and not getting too close to Baskets and Baskets because they didn't want to get hit by a Frisbee.

They asked Toomey how business was and he said it was pretty good.

They watched Rosa, the new girl, make a beautiful grab with her right hand at a high one and a tactical move with her left to keep the area around the upper chest from coming uncovered.

Toomey called, "Good move, Rosa." And his two companions applauded.

"How's business with you people?" Toomey asked.

Mort said it was good. Brinkman wasn't listening.

"I would think so," Toomey said. "With Christian Bounty buying up everything."

Mort nodded. "Lots of activity in the real estate market these days."

They took time to watch Helen catch a low one just off the ground.

Brinkman shook his head in admiration and envy and said to Toomey, "You sure know how to pick 'em."

"Far as I know," Toomey said, "they all come that way."

They watched for another minute or two, then Toomey said he had to go and went into the shop.

There was a message on his desk saying that Judge Lanahan had called and had left word for Toomey to call him.

So he did.

Judge Lanahan asked if he'd heard from Angela and he said he hadn't but that he expected to any day now.

"Do you know anyone who has heard from her?"

He said, "No. She never tells anyone where she is. That would ruin everything. She just shows up and joins in the happiness that she's come back safe and sound."

The judge apparently thought that over in silence for a few moments. Then he said, "If she isn't back by the end of this week I'm going to have to report her as a missing person. And send

187

out an all-state alarm. In fact, I think all of us would be subject to criticism for not having done that some time ago."

He sounded worried. Toomey tried to make him feel better. "She'll be back," he said. "I feel certain of that."

Judge Lanahan said he certainly hoped so. But if she wasn't back before the end of the week, he'd have to alert the state police.

Toomey agreed to that. And they said good-bye and hung up. And Toomey went out to the shop and wove some baskets to get his mind off things and heard eight of the top forty tunes most popular that week in WFRM land.

Toomey called his sister, Ethel, on the phone that night just to make sure Indiana was still there. He asked how things were going in Angora, and she said things hadn't changed much since he'd called a week ago.

"I'm thinking of coming out for a week just to see if I feel I might enjoy living there again."

She said, "If you enjoy living where you are, you'll enjoy living here."

Toomey liked that. She had always had a way of succinctly making a profound statement that Toomey admired.

"That's good, Ethel. I can tell that you're in a good humor tonight."

"If you're coming out here just to make sure the liquor stores haven't been closed down, I can save you a trip.

"They're still open."

"That doesn't worry me," Toomey said. "I'm not drinking much anymore."

She said, "If you're wondering if we still got crazy people who need psychoanalysis, quit worrying. We got two running for mayor in November and six for the school board. Just to mention the ones who come to mind right away."

"Eight would be enough for a start."

"As for the fishing, my girls think it's great. My two youngest went to the lake Saturday and both came home with new boyfriends."

"That's pretty good."

"One of the boys even has a job."

"That's even better."

She said, "Being employed may not be unusual where you are, but here in Angora it's newsworthy."

She was only partly joking. Angora had never been noted for its employment opportunities. Someone said that there had been a factory in the town once, but the man who had reported that fact was quite old and his memory wasn't very reliable.

"Sometimes I wonder how much the town has changed since I grew up there. I wonder if the kids still play baseball Saturday mornings in the vacant lot behind the old Cruft warehouse."

She said, "The old Cruft warehouse was torn down years ago. But if there was a vacant lot there when you were growing up, I'm sure it's still there. And still vacant."

They shared a small laugh about that.

Then he told her that there was something that he'd had on his mind a lot in recent months.

"You remember Madeline Toomey? The psychic?"

She asked what was a psychic.

"You know, someone who can predict the future. Communicate with people who have died. That kind of thing."

Ethel said, "Madeline Toomey wasn't a psychic, for God's sake! She was a dressmaker. She used to pick up a little extra money telling fortunes to people with no brains and two dollars.

"You don't even remember her," she said. "She died before you were born."

"I know that," Toomey said. "She died a day or two before I was born."

He said, "I was named after her."

"That's right," she said. "What about it?"

He said, "Remember how people thought that maybe I had inherited her ability to predict people's futures?"

For a long moment or two there was silence from her end of the line. Then she said, "I don't remember anything about that. And I was seven or eight years old when she died. If anything had been said about that, I'd remember it."

"Well, I got the idea from someone," Toomey said. "In fact, one of the reasons I want to come back to Angora is to learn a little more about what Madeline Toomey was like."

"You didn't get that notion from me," she said. "Or from your mother."

Toomey said, "Well, I got it from somewhere. And I know she's been on my mind a lot in recent years."

He said, "I even feel I know what she looked like."

After a moment, he said, "She was small, wasn't she? Small and thin and kind of hunched over. Black hair. Sharp black eyes."

Ethel said, "No. Not that I remember."

And thought about it for a few seconds.

"I remember that she was small, but not thin. She was rather fat, actually, and had red hair. That I do remember. Dyed red hair."

Then she got a bit more worked up, as she had a tendency to do sometimes. She said, "Toomey, I think you've lost your mind!"

Then she said, "Look, Toomey. You remember Steven? Madeline's oldest boy?"

"Yes."

"Well, he's a chiropractor now and I go to see him about once every month or two."

Toomey didn't say anything.

"Sometimes we get talking about old times and that neighborhood we all grew up in. And he talks about how people used to come to his house to have his mother tell their fortunes. He still has her old crystal ball, in fact."

Then she said, "Wait a minute."

She was probably stubbing out a cigarette and taking another from the pack. He remembered it was one of the things she did when she got agitated about something. Chain-smoked.

She was back on. "He always speaks of his mother with real affection. Thought she was a great person. But she couldn't predict the future any more than you or I could."

Toomey didn't accept that. He said, "People wouldn't have kept going to her if she hadn't been of some help to them."

"That's not necessarily true, Toomey. You should know that."

190

Then she said, "Anyway, Steve remembers her as a nice, lovable fraud. People liked her. And maybe some of them got some help from her. But Steven says that she couldn't predict rain if the sky turned black and it started to thunder and lightning."

Toomey said, "Okay, okay. I'm sure Steve would know."

He said, "I was just curious, that's all."

Then he said he had to go. "But I wish you'd cut down on your smoking. You always smoke a lot when you get worked up about something."

She said that she hadn't had a cigarette for six months. "I had some water boiling a minute ago and had to go turn it off."

She suggested once more that he lay off the drinking and he told her he'd practically cut it out entirely.

"And I wish you'd get out of that foolish basket business. I'm tired of having to lie to people when they ask me how you're doing these days."

He said, "Just tell them I'm practicing in a small town in western Massachusetts. You don't need to tell them what I'm practicing."

Before they hung up she said, "Sometimes I worry about you. I wish you'd come for a visit before long. I think you're either drinking too much, working too hard, or staying out in the sun too long."

None of those things, he told her. But he promised he'd give her suggestion some serious thought.

"It would be good for me, I know. I'll call you back before long and let you know when I can make it."

She said once again that they had plenty of room and that everyone would like to see him.

He fixed himself a very small drink and talked to Roman about it.

Every time he mentioned the wide, flat countryside, cornfields, sycamore trees, the muddy clay-colored creeks and the broad, slow-moving rivers, Roman thumped his tail.

So he called Ethel back and said he could make it.

"How about next week?"

She liked that. She said that she had mentioned to the girls that he might be coming soon and they were delighted. And she had told Ed. He'd said, great! They'd find something to shoot, even if it was only clay pigeons.

At the very time that Ethel was telling Toomey that she wished he'd get out of the basket business, several people in the poolroom of the Munsen post of the Veterans of Foreign Wars were saying practically the same thing.

Bud Dawson and a friend were having a friendly game of eight ball for a bottle of beer. And Bud had run three balls in a row.

A moment before he had casually mentioned to his friends that his wife, Kate, had taken the kids and gone back to her mother.

He chalked his cue and studied the next shot.

"Wednesday was her birthday and I offered to take her out to dinner, but she preferred to go out with her friend, Lorraine LeClair. So I let her. What the hell. If that's what she wants."

The only shot he had was the fourteen ball. He studied it a moment.

"So she leaves the kids with her mother and goes out to dinner."

The fourteen was a tough shot. But the only shot he had.

"She doesn't get home until three in the morning. Loaded. And bringing in a big wicker basket that she said that guy Bougereau had made for her."

He chalked the cue vigorously for a few seconds.

"So the first thing I do is take the goddamn basket out to the backyard and put the ax to it."

There was very little of the fourteen showing, but he hit it just right and cut it neatly into the corner pocket.

Marty Johnson, the fellow he was playing against, pounded the bottom of his stick hard against the floor several times.

"Damn good shot!" Marty said. And the others who were watching said the same thing.

"Then I came in and showed her that no wife of mine lets some man give her things." And he picked up the chalk again.

He didn't include in the story the part about how he had

dragged her into the bedroom and told her he was going to make love to her whether she wanted to or not, and she didn't want to and he had had to tear her clothes off and slap her around a bit before she'd do it. But he'd done it, and it sure as hell wasn't bad.

Marty Johnson said, "Just don't leave bruises."

The eleven ball was a straight shot and he made it easily. And picked up the chalk again.

"Nothing wrong with a few bruises," Bud said. "Helps them remember."

He took a moment to study the eight ball shot. Then moved a few steps to his right to look at it from another angle.

"I'll give her two more days to come back. If she's not back by Saturday, I'll go up to her mother's and take the kids out and bring them home."

He moved back to his original position. And shook his head. That was a scratch shot if ever there was one.

Marty said, "Something's got to be done about that Bougereau person." And a few of the watchers echoed that thought.

Then Marty took the cube of chalk at his end of the table and ran it across his cue tip to show that in his opinion the game wasn't over because Bud wouldn't dare try that shot because he'd scratch if he did.

A little poolroom strategy.

Someone said, "I'll tell you what I think we ought to do."

Marty said, "What?"

The man said, "I think a few of us ought to go up there some night this week and ask Bougereau about making a donation to the VFW building fund. And try to get him to say something we don't like. And we get mad and work him over a little."

There was enthusiastic agreement with that idea. Then silence, so Bud could make his shot.

What he was afraid would happen, happened. The eight ball sank into the left side pocket, as planned, but the white ball bounced gently off the rail and with tantalizing slowness rolled up to the lip of the right corner pocket.

And dropped in.

Dawson let out a yell and a curse and stomped his foot hard on the floor. And threw his cue stick across the room.

21

Friday morning started off well enough.

Toomey woke up early, couldn't get back to sleep right away, so he got up and went fishing for an hour. Caught two bass big enough to keep, both over fourteen inches long. He got them on a gray artificial mouse at the edge of the lily pads just the other side of where the long tree trunk runs into the water. Cleaned them both, had one for breakfast, and still got to the office by a little after nine o'clock.

Angela called about nine-thirty. Collect, of course.

He told the operator that he would accept the collect call, then said, "Hi!"

She said, "Hi!"

"How is everything?"

"All right."

"Where are you?" Then before she had a chance to answer

he said quickly, "It's somewhere in New Jersey, isn't it?"

She said no. She was in West Jefferson, Ohio. "It's near Columbus."

Toomey said, "Oh. I think I know the place."

He said, "There's a miniature golf course at the edge of town, isn't there?"

She thought so.

"And right next to that is a Burger Heaven?"

She didn't know.

"I know the place well," Toomey said. "I've passed through there many times."

She didn't say anything in response to that.

"But all that's beside the point," Toomey said. "What's on your mind?"

She said, "I need the money you owe me."

"All right. Do you remember offhand how much I owe you?"

"A day and a half pay."

"I'll send two day's pay," Toomey said. "Just tell me where to send the check."

She gave him the name of the motel and the address.

"What's the zip code?"

She didn't know that.

"I need the money in a hurry."

He told her that he would put the check in the mail today. Special delivery.

"Are you all right?"

"Sure."

"How do you like Ohio?"

She said that she didn't. And he said that he was sorry to hear that.

"If you want to hold a minute," he said, "I'll see if there are any messages or mail for you."

He unwrapped a cigar, lit it, tossed the match away.

"I don't find any mail for you," he said, "but I see here that I made a note to myself to remind you that your father called. Said that he needed to get in touch with you right away."

"What about?"

196

Toomey said, "Angela, how would I know what your father wants to talk to you about?"

He said, "I will say this, though, that he sounded as if it were something very important. Like maybe he'd won the lottery or something. Or been appointed ambassador to France. Or maybe you'd just inherited a lot of money from a rich uncle."

He asked, "Do you have a rich uncle?"

From the pause on her end, he suspected that she did have one. On her mother's side.

"Yes."

"Well," Toomey said, "I'm not saying that that is why he wanted to reach you. I just made up that part. But I do know that he wanted to hear from you right away."

He asked, "Do you have his number?"

"Yes."

"And your mother's number? In case you can't reach your father?"

"Yes."

"Will you call them right now, before you forget?"

"I'll call them right now."

"Good," he said. "And take care of yourself, will you?"

She said that she would. And they both said good-bye and hung up.

He pushed the phone to one side, then went out into the shop and told everyone that Angela had just called from West Jefferson, Ohio, and that she was fine and had said to tell everyone hello.

They were glad to hear that and everyone asked if she was going to be coming back to Munsen and he said he didn't know. She was having a good time in Ohio and might stay there a while longer.

The first time that Mrs. Murphey came into the office he mentioned to her that he had decided to go on vacation for a week or more and asked if she thought she could handle things while he was away.

She said that she could, of course. And for him to go and

197

have a good time. And not worry about anything.

"I'm going to leave early this evening. As soon as I can after work. And drive all night."

He said, "Going to or from Indiana you always drive all night. It's traditional."

The expression on her face showed that she didn't approve of that.

"Why don't you get a good night's sleep and leave early in the morning?"

"You don't do it that way," he said. "You always leave right after work and drive until you get there."

She looked disappointed. She said, "That's too bad. My daughter's coming this evening to pick up Myra. And I know that she's been wanting to meet you."

That made Toomey stop and think for a moment. Almost made him change his mind.

But he remembered something that Maggie O'Reilly had told him. And it scared him a little.

Already he practically loved Myra's mother, and he hadn't even met her yet. You could be pretty sure what would happen if she came to visit him. Unless she kicked his dog and spit on the floor, he'd end up proposing to her before the evening was over.

The only intelligent thing for him to do until he got his feelings about women under better control was to avoid them.

Maggie would have agreed with that.

"Now that I've decided to go," he said, "I want to get started as soon as I can."

She looked quite unhappy about that decision, and that made Toomey feel bad.

"When I get back," he said, "I think you ought to take a vacation yourself. A two-week paid vacation would be good for you."

That idea cheered her up a little. But she was still unhappy about his not getting to meet her daughter. And as she was leaving he almost changed his mind and said he'd stay long enough to meet her daughter.

But he didn't.

It was a long day.

In midmorning he took Roman and Myra to Harvey's for ice cream. Then on to the post office to mail Angela's check to her.

He chatted a while with Mrs. Blanchard, the postmistress. She wasn't one of his admirers, having heard so much about what was probably going on with him and his half-clad women workers, but he told her he thought she was looking good and asked how her garden was coming. And her grandchildren? Things like that.

Back at the office he heard that Judge Lanahan's secretary had called to say that they had heard from Angela and that she was well.

Good.

During the afternoon he spent some time making baskets and listening to the new girl tell about her astral travels. She said the trips were always scary. And everyone said they didn't know why she went on them if they were scary. And Sarah told about how she was even afraid to go up in an airplane.

He heard more of the top forty tunes on the radio but they all sounded like the top forty of last week and someone said that they were.

They asked him what he was going to do on his vacation and he said go fishing and play miniature golf. And they asked what was miniature golf.

At the end of the day, the girls all came into his office and told him to have a good time and to say that they wished they were going with him.

He said he wished they were, too.

Then it was time to say good-bye to Myra and that wasn't very much fun.

"Tell Toomey good-bye," Mrs. Murphey said, "because it will be a long time before you'll see him again."

He wished she hadn't said that. But it was too late.

Myra started to cry.

"Her mother said that the day-care center will be opening

up again Monday, so Myra will be staying over there for the next few weeks.

"And she'll be in kindergarten in September, so she probably won't be back here again until next summer. Except maybe to visit for a day or so."

Myra was crying harder now, and Toomey wasn't far from it himself.

But he told her that if she didn't get back to see him, he'd go over there to see her.

He told her about how he and Roman would come to see her and how they'd all have a good time. And that he wanted her to take all the crayon books back with her and fill them up to show him when he came to see her and that he'd send her more when those were finished. And that every once in a while he'd mail her a batch of pencils to sharpen for him.

None of that made her feel much better, but after a while she stopped crying.

Then they were gone, and Toomey had the chance to cry if he wanted to. And he almost did.

He poured a drink into the paper cup, so small a drink that it wouldn't have filled an eyedropper.

Then he poured one more, but it was even smaller.

And turned off the lights, locked the doors, and went back to his house to pack.

And so it goes.

Life's like that.

Tears as well as laughter. Pain along with the joy. You hear people say good-bye about as often as you hear them say hello, it seems.

Water runs downhill, taxes go up, and sooner or later everyone has a line drawn through his or her name on some list somewhere.

Mrs. Estey gets a call from her husband, who says that he has to work late again.

"That's too bad." And she tells him that she thinks he's been working too hard lately. Besides, she's fixed a big dinner. Especially for him. "Can't it wait until Monday?"

He says that it can't. And not to expect him until late.

After they hang up she dials the number the truck driver had left with her.

Mrs. Malloy gets everything ready for her husband's birthday dinner and when his car pulls into the driveway the kids go running out to meet him and he hugs everybody and after dinner they bring in the cake and everyone sings "Happy Birthday to You."

That night all of them go to an outdoor movie and have popcorn and soda and anything else anyone wants.

In Boston, that elderly statesman with the attractive young secretary gets back from the floor of the Senate and locks the door so they won't be interrupted. But the young woman tells him he might just as well unlock it because she's not going to do that anymore.

Also, she's thinking very seriously about writing a book about what goes on on Beacon Hill.

She has been talking to a friend who is a writer and would help her with it. And she thinks she's going to call the book *Behind Closed Doors*.

In Washington, D.C., that young and impetuous aide to the President finally gets his chance to lay that certain young female member of the household staff across that one particular bed in the White House upon which so many a famous personage has lain before. Hurriedly, of course. But now, at last, they have a story to tell that will stop conversation in any bar or cocktail party from Maine to California.

And they're caught.

In Farmington, the wife of the mayor left the country club with her daughter and headed for home. She was an attractive woman, in her late thirties, blond, still shapely, wearing a two-piece bathing suit and not at all unaware that she still got admiring glances from the males as she drove through town in her red Mustang convertible.

Her daughter, eighteen years old, sitting next to her, was even more beautiful. She got not only admiring glances but long, low whistles. But neither of them was offended. Sometimes they turned and looked at each other and smiled.

It was all rather amusing, until, on South Main Street, where they stopped for a red light, and five men on motorcycles pulled alongside.

They, too, made it clear that they appreciated good-looking women with long blond hair and tanned bare skin. But the language they used to demonstrate their good taste was crude and insulting. They looked mean and in an ugly mood. Two were large with long blond hair that spilled out from under their helmets, looking so much alike that she assumed they were brothers. One was slender with a long red scar across his cheek. The other two were black.

The one who had stopped alongside her looked across her and at her daughter's legs and bare midriff and whistled and grinned. His companions offered their own opinions. All of which were favorable. And she was suddenly afraid as well as angry.

She told the one nearest her to *move off*. In response, he shifted his look from the daughter to her and let his glance go slowly from her shoulders down to her legs. And grinned. He even rested his arm on the door of her car.

She hit at it and waited for the light to change.

"What's the matter, lady? Don't you like people looking at your legs?"

The goddamn light was still red.

She took the cigarette she was smoking and very calmly reached over and put the lighted end down on the back of the man's hand and was pleased to hear him scream in pain.

Just as the light changed, the man moved his bike ahead a few feet, and with a sharp ring on his right hand scratched a deep X on the hood of the car. And looked back at her and spit. And as her car leaped ahead she heard him call her a bitch and saw him rake the side of the car with a long scratch.

There was a police car in the next block. She pulled alongside it and motioned for the officer to pull over to the curb. They stopped. The officer got out, came to her car, and she identified herself and showed him what had happened.

He got on the radio right away. Then took off after them.

At Christian Bounty things were more peaceful. Three men sat around a table, finishing their coffee. They had been talking about how good it would be if they owned Baskets and Baskets and could offer employment to some of their students and staff who needed to work.

One said, "Why don't we buy the business?"

Another said, "Let's ask our lawyer to get in touch with him and see if he's interested in selling. Ask him how much he wants."

The first said, "It's too early for that. We don't need to let him know we're interested in the business. All we need to do is just buy the building and, after he's gone, take up where he left off."

He said, "There's no special skill involved in making baskets. The only information we need is the name of the wholesaler he sells the baskets to. And prices. That kind of thing. And he'd probably tell you all that for free, if you asked him."

He was right. The other two nodded their heads.

One suggested that they call him and make an appointment to see him.

But the one who had done most of the talking shook his head.

"I think we should just drop in on him. The three of us. Just stop in and talk to him. Tell him it's just a friendly visit."

He spoke as if he had a good psychological reason for wanting to do it that way. So the other two went along with him.

"Why don't we go see him this evening? Right now is as good a time as any."

That made sense. So they did it.

In Farmington, at the county jail, Sheriff Holmes said, "Shit!" And knew that there was going to be trouble again.

Every time a prisoner escapes from a work detail, everyone in town who can get his hands on a pencil and a piece of paper writes to the newspaper and says that the prisoner work-release program is a menace, and that because prisoners are allowed to work off the grounds during the day the women and children of Farmington are not safe.

Three days from now, anyone reading the letters to the editor in the *Farmington Courrier* will believe that everyone in town is cowering in his home, behind locked doors, and will remain that way until this dangerous and impractical program is stopped.

"Who was it who didn't report back?"

"John Weinert."

Holmes shook his head.

"The dumb bastard. He had less than a month to serve."

He swore a few more times.

"What's the story behind it?"

"His friends here say he probably took off because word had got back to him that his wife was planning to take off with the kids. And running around with a man."

There was no way of knowing whether that was true or not. In jail, like everywhere else, there are always some people who will feel better by making someone else feel worse. It always just so happens that someone learns from someone else that a certain prisoner's wife is running around with a man while her husband is in jail. A black man, usually, if the prisoner is white. And vice versa.

That's part of being in jail.

"Do you know where his wife's living?"

The deputy's name was Perry. He was tall, thin, old, and tired of his job. If all the prisoners ran away and none was ever found again, that would be all right with him.

"Somewhere in Munsen. And working at a place called Baskets and Baskets. That's all we know."

"Is she maybe living with the man who owns the place, or something?"

"That's what Weinert was told," Perry said. "If not living with him, at least running around with him."

Holmes swore one more time, sighed deeply, and leaned back in his chair.

"So send a couple men down to the baskets place to check it

out. And tell the owner Weinert's probably picked up a gun by now and that he's dangerous."

Sandy Sumner, short, stocky, freckles and golden-red hair, eighteen years old and just finishing her first week of work, left the Farmington General Hospital and headed home. Back to her parents' home, that is. In Mumford. She had only a furnished room in Farmington, no car, and no money. Next week, however, she would get her first check, then more checks in coming weeks, and before long an apartment of her own and a car. But until that time when she could buy a car, there was no way to get home except hitchhike. So that was what she did.

It was not the first time she had hitchhiked. But it turned out to be the most exciting one.

She got a ride as far as Munsen with a woman who was pregnant and who said that she was an automobile mechanic. And in Munsen she got a ride with a man named Marty Johnson. He was with three friends from the VFW and they had come to see a man about something. After picking her up, Marty had tried to talk her into going to have a drink with him and his friends, but she refused. Still, he had driven her to Mumford anyway. Eight miles out of his way.

She had a date with him for tomorrow night. He didn't really turn her on, but she wasn't going out with anyone else right now and he had said he'd like to take her to dinner. And dancing. Which would be fun.

The woman who said she was an automobile mechanic was named Toni Heller. She was on her way to her mother's in Munsen for the weekend.

Sandy liked to talk, so she told the woman about her new job as a nurse's aide and why she was hitchhiking and that she was going to get a car as soon as she could afford it. Within a few weeks, she hoped. And that once she got to know people in Farmington she probably wouldn't be going back to Mumford very often.

There wasn't anything happening in Mumford, so why go back there?

When she told the woman that she worked in a hospital, the

woman said that her uncle back in Coultraine, where she lived
and worked, was going into the hospital there on Sunday and
was going to be operated on on Monday. She said that he had
cancer and the doctor had told her that he was afraid her uncle
had put off too long doing something about it. He might not be
able to go back to work, even. And would probably have to sell
the garage.

Sandy asked the woman if she thought she'd be able to keep
her job, and she said that she didn't know.

Depended upon who bought the business.

Sandy was glad she wasn't as old as that woman and pregnant and worried about losing her job.

She wondered if Mrs. Heller's husband worked. Or if maybe
she was divorced. But didn't want to ask.

Toomey was in the kitchen making sandwiches. He remembered that, back when he was a child, while his father was still
around, whenever the family went to visit relatives or friends
more than two hours away, his mother always made a lot of
sandwiches.

"One thing I want to warn you about," he said, "is the
rabbits."

Roman thumped his tail on the floor once or twice to show
that he was listening.

"Even the ones in the middle of town are tough enough to
scare away most dogs. Except German shepherds and Dober-
man pinschers."

He finished making the third ham sandwich. Which should
be enough.

"But they get tougher the farther out you go." And he put
the sandwiches, wrapped in waxed paper, into a brown paper
bag.

"And my sister," he said, "lives in the last house on the last
street in town."

He wrapped up the scraps to take along for Roman.

All this wrapping of scraps and making of sandwiches
turned out to be a waste of time.

Mrs. Blanchard, the town postmistress, heard the motorcycles pull around the building and into the parking lot in back. The post office was closed now, of course, but Mrs. Blanchard lived in the back half of the building. She saw them, the five of them, each one more mean-looking than all the others, take off their helmets and start talking about something. Then one pulled out a small bottle, took a drink from it, then passed it along to the others.

That made her very angry.

She didn't fool with the local police. She called the state police, only two miles away. And told Sergeant Maloney, whom she knew personally, to get a car over here right away.

Sandy noticed that Mrs. Heller slowed down as they got into town and at one place looked as if she was about to stop. Then sped up again.

Sandy said, "You don't need to go out of your way."

The woman said, "My mother lives down that street we just passed. But I'm going to take you another mile or so to where you can pick up Route 24. Which will take you right into Mumford, as you know."

That was nice of her. Sandy told her so.

"No problem," she said. "I have time."

She said that she'd never been to Mumford, although she knew where it was.

"It's even smaller than Munsen," Sandy said. "Nothing ever happens there."

The woman laughed and said, "Nothing ever happens here, either."

Then the woman said, "Damn!" And slowed down. And looked into the rearview mirror.

Sandy looked back. There was a police car coming, its blue light flashing.

The woman slowed down even more and pulled over to the right. And the police car caught up with them.

Then kept on going.

The woman looked relieved. She said, "I thought he was after me."

Up ahead Sandy saw a police car coming from that direction, too. Blue lights. Sirens.

Two of them.

Sandy said, "Something's happened."

Cars ahead of them were slowing down, pulling over to the side.

The woman said, "I guess there's been an accident."

Another police car passed them from behind. But this one wasn't using its lights or siren.

Sandy saw on the right a long low building with a sign in front that said Baskets and Baskets. And just beyond that a small brown-shingled cottage.

It was there that something had happened.

There were motorcycles at the curb, and five or six men in black jackets were standing in a line facing the house. And in front of the house, confronting them, was a large man holding a dog by the collar with one hand and gripping what looked like a baseball bat in the other.

Then she heard the woman scream, and the car came to such a quick stop that Sandy hit her head against the windshield. But before she even had time to complain about that, the woman was out of the car and running toward the line of men.

Sandy saw her stop and pick up a rock and throw it toward one of the men in black jackets. But by now they had turned to face the police who were moving toward them. And the woman got a very indignant look from one of the motorcyclists.

What did she think she was doing?

And by now Sandy was out of the car and moving closer to see what was going on.

This was one of the craziest sights Sandy had ever seen.

All those people there at one time! Police cars, other cars full of people, and men on motorcycles. Everyone milling around looking at one another.

Later, when Marty and his friends were driving her to Mumford, it was all they talked about. All those people.

Marty said he'd learned that one of the police cars was from

Farmington and had been after the motorcyclists. And the car from the county sheriff's office had been there looking for someone who had escaped from jail that day. And had found him. Behind the building.

The state police were there, but Marty hadn't been able to find out why. One of his friends said that probably they had picked up on the radio word that there was trouble of some kind in town.

Marty said that the three men in the yellow Chevy were from Christian Bounty. You could tell by the bumper sticker. And no one had any idea why they were there.

The last police car to arrive, according to Marty, belonged to Nicocci, the chief of police. He hadn't even known there was any trouble. He'd stopped by to see if the fellow who owned Baskets and Baskets wanted to go fishing with him.

After Sandy watched the police take away the weapons the motorcyclists were carrying, things like chains and clubs, she looked around to see where Mrs. Heller was.

And this was the craziest part of the whole thing.

The woman she'd been riding with, the tall, pregnant, dark-haired woman who had said she was an auto mechanic and lived in Coultraine and maybe was about to lose her job at the garage, was standing over by the door to the cottage with the big man and his dog, and the man had his arms around her and was hugging her and she had her arms around him, too. And it looked like the woman was crying.

And the man, too.

22

When the kid was born, one thing everyone agreed on was that they wouldn't call him Toomey, after his father. Mrs. Murphey said she had never known anyone in her life called Junior she could stand to have around.

They could have called him Tommy, obliquely named after his father, but that would have been cute and Toomey said that he'd never known a lineman with a cute name who could open up a hole wide enough to drive a ten-speed bike through.

Besides, Toni said she had already decided what to call the boy. She was going to name him after a man she had met early in December last year on the Massachusetts Turnpike.

So they called him George. George Bougereau.

Toomey said that if they had another child and it was a girl, he wanted to call it Maggie O'Reilly Bougereau.

Christian Bounty didn't buy the building after all. So Mrs.

Murphey took over the business. She said that she planned to run it pretty much the way it had been run before. She wanted to continue hiring young women who needed some money to get them through some temporary difficulty.

The only innovation she had in mind, as far as the hiring of workers was concerned, was that she was going to try to have a better conversational balance. She and Toomey recalled that once they had had a young woman who was into organic gardening and ecology, and how much everyone had learned from her.

Toni said, "Someone with a literary background would add a lot. Like maybe a former librarian trying to make a little money while she was working on a novel."

That was a good idea.

Her mother liked that very much. She said, "We could have the kind of place that would be an educational experience as well as a chance to make a little money."

"Maybe," Toomey said, "you could even get a government grant."

Toni said, "People wouldn't just leave, they'd graduate."

So much for that.

Toomey still hadn't made that trip to Indiana.

He had called Ethel that night to say that he'd changed his plans and wouldn't be out there the next day. Then a week later he had called to say that he'd be out there in early November with his wife and two kids. And that was fine with her. The fishing is never good in November, of course, but Ed would know where they could go shoot some pheasants.

She told him that only a couple days ago she had happened to be talking to Steven Toomey, Madeline's oldest son, the chiropractor, and she had told Steven that Toomey was coming for a visit soon. And he, strangely enough, had said that Toomey had been on his mind lately.

"Steven said that for some reason he'd had the feeling that everything was going to start going well for you pretty soon and that you'd be settled down, happily married, and raising some happy children."

"Did he say how many children there were going to be?"

She said, "Toomey, of course not. He wouldn't know anything about that."

Toomey said, "Tell him I said hello."

She said she would.

"And tell him," Toomey said, "that if he'd ever be willing to sell that old crystal ball his mother used, I'd like to buy it."

She said she'd mention that to him.

Toomey had kept the old blue van. It would be good to have it to use on weekend picnics or fishing or for trips to Brown County in the fall to see the foliage.

They loaded up the van one brisk morning in the first week of November, said good-bye to everyone in the shop, put Roman in the back and George in his basket on the front seat.

Toni said, "I'd like to drive."

"Are you sure you're strong enough?"

She said, "For Christ's sake, yes!"

He said, "Okay! Okay!" And tossed the last suitcase in. And the bags of sandwiches and cookies.

"Myra can sit on my lap."

As Toni drove him out of town they spotted a few people they knew.

Charlie Nelson, who owns the grocery store on Main Street, was sweeping the sidewalk. And he waved. Which was nice.

And Mr. Collins was coming out of the post office as they passed by, starting his appointed rounds, shouldering his bulky bag of mail like some reluctant Santa Claus.

He saw them and waved and they waved back.

Harvey was in front of his store, talking to Nick Nicocci.

Both of them waved.

Toni honked. Toomey waved.

And they headed west.